First Person

Eddie McGarrity

ISBN: 1495232948
ISBN-13: 978-1495232947

DEDICATION

For Colin Parker
sail on, silver mug

CONTENTS

Eddie McGarrity

ACKNOWLEDGMENTS

Cover image © 2014 Gavin Campbell
Reproduced by kind permission

THE GREEN ROOM

EYEBROWS LIFT BEFORE I can even move my eyelids, which flicker open to reveal only darkness. I'm lying on my arms and move to release them but I'm stuck. My fingers tingle and, from the right pinkie to the wrist, my hand feels numb and meaty. To get the circulation going, I flex my hand and it rubs in soft earth. The ground I'm on feels warm and dry. I open and close my mouth, my tongue searching for some moisture. Twisting my head I see a faint ragged circle of light behind me, an opening of some kind, which leads to where I am. I can't see a ceiling. And then it hits me. I'm lying on my back, under the ground, and I start to panic.

I can feel dread growing inside me. My feet start to kick at loose dirt and it's only when I connect with something hard that I realise I can move my legs freely. The movement has shifted me slightly and I move onto my side, relieving some pressure on my arms, which I now realise are held by rope scraping at the wrists. I can only move my fingers. Panic subsides when I realise I'm breathing cool air wafting in from the far away circle of light.

Figuring it must be the way out of this underground chamber, I start to shuffle. Kicking again strike the same hard surface. It gives a dull thud but it gives me some purchase to sit up slightly. Moving gingerly in case I hit my head on an unseen ceiling, I struggle my way into a kneeling position to find there is actually quite a bit of room. It's only when I try to stand, that my head hits strands of loose dirt which patters down around me, clinging to my sweaty face. Some of it lands in my already dry mouth. I manage to tongue it out and look around.

Meagre light from the opening shows a rough-cut tunnel which leads to this area, like a burrow made just big enough for a man. I try to think how I got here, remembering only nodding off on the bus, which I normally do on the way home from work. Dread fills my gut again. Daring only to glance at the opening, I know the only way for me is to go there to it. I've either been put here for some purpose, or something awaits me at the tunnel's edge. Already my shins are hurting from kneeling, but I make to move forward, one knee at a time.

Pale green light rises behind me, lifting the gloom. It stops me. Anxiety slumps my shoulders. My tie is missing and the top button of my white short-sleeved shirt has been undone. It does help me breathe though. Whoever put me here has thought of this. I dare not look over my shoulder. I force my eyes to keep focused on the opening in front of me and imagine the cool freedom beyond. Fear of not turning is too great and I'm forced to turn away from the opening and confront the green light behind me.

I see a room. Its normality shocks me and I shuffle round on my knees, as best I can with hands still tightly bound behind me. Dragging thin trousers through granules of dirt, I come closer to the room and see now what my feet kicked against. A thick glass wall separates me from the room. My breath, coming shallow and fast, mists it slightly and I move head and shoulders to take in all the details.

Beyond the glass is a pretty little room, perhaps for a girl, but old-fashioned, like something from long ago. A short fluffy bed, strewn with a shiny blanket, is over to my left. To my right is a four drawer chest. Despite the green haze I can see the furniture is white, though the paint is chipped, and golden flowers around the corners are worn and smooth.

The hypnotic green light is from a bulb set into the wall above the bed. Between the bed and drawers is a dark doorway, framed by glossy wood. It is set into the wall, which is covered in faded flower wallpaper. Something coalesces in the doorway, its outline emerging from the shadows as it comes forward. I've stopped breathing. Elegant and slow, the outline resolves into that of a young woman. That gets me breathing and I fall back off my knees, gasping in fright.

I see the woman step out of the doorway, her golden hair is floating in the air. She seems to fall into the room and I see that she herself is floating. Her feet are off the floorboards as she drifts into the room. Eyes closed, her arms are lifeless and raised at the elbows, fingers curled in a resting position. I see now that she is followed by little pieces of debris which float alongside her. She is floating in water, with debris tumbling in her wake. I move to my knees again and scurry forward to the glass.

Made green in the light, she wears a blue dress, buttoned to the neck and flouncing out to her feet, which are in neat shoes. A small apron is fastened at her waist. I'm reminded of a viewing room in a resort swimming pool as she continues her movement. She remains straight backed but her head is dropping down as she floats towards me. Perched on her head, a tiny tiara glitters. She is getting closer. Her face is young but the skin is puffed and slack like that of a specimen in a jar. Dread pulls at me again as I begin to wonder if the room beyond this glass is filled not with water but some kind of preserving fluid.

She bobs towards me. Her face is nearly at the glass. Half-expecting her eyes to open I watch her float right in front of me. My breath mists the glass. Her foot catches on the metal frame of the bed and her head plinks on the surface, pushing her back onto her feet, which in turn pushes her back to the glass. This time the tiara touches. A tiny jewel scrapes on the glass and leaves a mark. The sound is almost nothing where I am, but I can see it happen.

She bobs again. The tiny jewel, a diamond, strikes the glass again. And again. A spider-like crack begins to spread.

TIMED OUT

MID-WINTER SUNSHINE threads through cold air and reaches me from between stripped branches as I step carefully through long pale grass. The ground beneath is soft despite the chilled air and time of year. My boots compress yellowing stems of grass into damp earth. I sniff. I can feel my nose numbing. It is probably already red. There is no smell in the air, save the damp boggy terrain, though for a moment I think I can smell the remnants of cigarette smoke, but then it is gone. The air is so still, I believe, that there would have been a man standing here minutes ago smoking and the smell of nicotine and tar has clung to this spot like a fragrant memory.

My hands are in gloves and I wear a thick coat. I feel myself heating up with the exertion. I take off my hat, fold it up, and put it into a coat pocket. The cold air instantly attacks my damp head as the sweat evaporates.

I stand in a landscape shaped like a massive natural flat bottomed bowl. In the distance, all around me are low hills forming a horizon that means it will get dark sooner than if the topography had been fully flat. It is already half past two in the afternoon. It has taken all day to get here. Across the vale, limp grasses are punctuated by groups of dense trees, bare of all leaves. I pass from the filtered shadows of one of the groups of trees as I walk. I do not hear any birds. I am heading for a building on the other side of a line of trees. I cannot yet see it, but I know it is there. I have not been here in many years and hope, that even though it was a ruin when I was a boy, it will still be there. I keep moving towards the line of trees. I stride confidently, purposefully.

Often I have recurring dreams that are like an episodic story. Each night's instalment picks up from the previous one. Though the episodes can sometimes be separated by years, they form a narrative in my head, and I can follow the story. Even if, during my wakened state, I had completely forgotten the dream, my unconscious mind can pick up the strands. It is like watching a soap opera on TV where even if you miss a few episodes you can still understand the plot on your return. My dreams contain almost the same amount of sadness, loss, and pain as a soap opera, although I do not live my life like a soap opera. I would never leave the house to cross the street to buy a cup of coffee. What I do is listen to my dreams, and try to decode their meaning. This is why I am here. I have had a dream about this place. I have a mission.

Many years ago, when I was a boy, I lived not far from here. I liked the scenery in winter; the quietness; the solitude. My favourite spot was the ruined control tower. There had been an airfield here during the war, and there had been many buildings, but the control tower was the only thing that was left. During the war they would have called it an aerodrome and, unlike many other wartime aerodromes, it did not become a commercial airport, but instead became a ruin. As a boy I imagined it in its glory and not just the thin shell of red bricks that was actually there. Using my imagination, I could see what it would have been like. You could still make out the tall windows on the upper storey, and you could imagine the spitfires and the tornadoes and the bombers taking off and landing here. I imagined my grand-father in the control tower, much younger, looking out of those tall windows through powerful binoculars as the spitfires and tornadoes and bombers took off and landed. I played there all the time but I dared not enter the tower. My grand-father told me the basement was dark, deep, and dangerous. I loved my grand-father. He was a wonderful man. I lived with him in his house until he died and when I became very sad I went to live somewhere else in another part of the country.

I approach the line of trees. Something catches my eye. It is brown and large, and has red parts. I ignore it for a moment as I approach the trees. This copse is thick but looking through I can see that I will be able to pick my way through fairly easily. There is a small barbed-wire fence I will have to negotiate, but it is broken and low, and I will be able to step over it easily. I do not remember this fence and am confused as to what boundary it might mark. I follow the line of the rusty wire to my left and catch sight of what I had noticed previously. It is a deer and, caught by its neck in the twisted barbed wire, it is dead. Birds have been pecking at exposed flesh. Strangely, the dark eyeballs remain untouched. They stare out queasily in motionless terror, rolled to the side showing a crescent white, a frozen moment in time like a photograph of a painful memory. The deer's head is twisted at an awkward angle. It must have struggled vainly to free itself. I feel ill, step over the fence, and keep moving.

Once, as a boy, I was playing near the abandoned control tower, imagining myself a squadron leader waiting for the call to scramble, when I heard a noise. It was a man running towards the tower. My memory of him shimmers into life as he came towards me. I was startled as he paused briefly to regard me with a puzzled look, before darting in the door and down the stairwell that led to the forbidden basement. My memory shimmers again as he darted out of sight. I never saw him return from the darkness.

I keep moving. Springy black moss-covered branches lick past me as I make my way through the trees. I could have gone round, but I prefer the adventure of clambering through the trees like a child. I have not done this since I fell ill as a teenager. I think of the deer, trapped in the fence, and wonder of the events in its life that brought it to that fence. If the deer had been human, and could see its destiny, I am sure it would have made different choices.

Despite the ongoing narrative of some of my dreams, there is one dream I have that recurs again and again. It is of that same mid-winter day when I was a boy and the strange man ran into the tower. In the dream I can hear another sound. It is a thin, frightened voice, calling out, "Help! Help!" For many years I thought it was the man who had become trapped in the forbidden basement and was crying out for help. The dream recurred over and over across many years. The man runs in, and then I hear the cry, like a voice calling out to me across time in a thin, frightened voice. Details in the dream were always the same. Until last week, I was sure of the events. My conscious memory told me that the man ran in and that was all, but my unconscious mind had created its own memory. Consulting books on the subject of dreams, I concluded that my juvenile anxiety about not seeing the man again meant I was concerned about his welfare. Therefore my unconscious had constructed a cry for assistance that reflected my own neurosis about the dark.

But now I was not so sure about the sequence of events. A new dream had happened where the sequence was different. Sleeping as normal in my own warm bed, I returned in my mind to this place. I was playing at war planes when I heard a thin, frightened voice call out, "Help! Help!" I felt a chill in dream, as my boyhood self froze on the spot. I could hear it again. "Help! Help!" The sound was emanating from the basement of the control tower, and for a moment, just a moment, it sounded familiar. Unable to move, I shuddered as I heard it again. "Help! Help!" I moved towards the control tower. At its base, a narrow doorway lay open to the elements. Rusted hinges showed where a wooden door would once have been. Cement steps inside the doorway led both up and down but I dared not move. This was a dream, of course, but it was terrifyingly real.

"Help! Help!" This time the voice was definitely familiar. It was me. I must have called out, to whom I could not know, but all of a sudden the man from my memory entered my dream. He shimmered and appeared in front of the boy me, and headed for the basement-leading steps at the inner doorway. He paused only briefly, to look down at me with a puzzled expression, before he shimmered again and disappeared.

I awoke in a terrible sweat. I could now no longer be sure of the sequence of events all those years ago. My dream had made me question everything. Perhaps the man who looked at me was puzzled because he could not understand why someone had ignored a plea for help. Immediately, I discharged myself and resolved to solve this mystery. I would return to the control tower and look for details of the events. I would investigate.

Not many people come here. It has taken me three hours and two buses and a one hour walk to get here. I am tired, and very warm, despite the cold December air. I remove my gloves and put them in my coat pocket as I emerge from the trees. It has been worth it. I can see the ruined aerodrome ahead. I am elated. The control tower is just as I remember it, even though I am now questioning my memories. My happy boyhood in this place has been like a lantern that I have carried with me on my journey to becoming a man. Childhood illuminates adulthood. Understand the boy and you will understand what motivates the man. What we do as children resonates through our adult life like a wind chime in an autumn breeze.

There is a breeze now. It is from the north, and brings chilled air across this depressed landscape, having rolled off the low hills in the distance. To my left, the sun dips its toe beyond the horizon as if testing how it would feel to be on the other side of the world. I feel the breeze moving through me, exhilarating me. I am alive. I feel sure the events of my life have led me here, to this spot, to reach my destiny. It is as if I am suddenly taller.

Heading towards the red-brick shell of the ruined control tower, I take in all the details. Nothing much has changed. Pale yellow grass grows a little longer, and the tarmac surface of the runway is more cracked, and weed-ridden, but the features are still recognisable. The red-brick shell of the control tower rises into the air. I see now that the roof is crumbling, but the structure still seems sound. Perhaps I will save up to buy this place and renovate the building. The tall windows would be a good vantage point to see for miles. I have never stepped inside the tower, but I imagine myself up there in renovated splendour, surveying the land with bakelite binoculars, visualising aeroplanes taking off and landing. I picture the sounds of spitfires and tornadoes and bombers in my mind, as I stretch out my senses into the chilly air, listening out for any real sounds. I remember I have not heard any birds since I got off the bus. Suddenly I stop.

I have heard something. I am sure of it, though I cannot be certain if I imagined it, or whether it was real. It was very faint, as if distant, or muffled, or below ground. It is something I have not heard for many years. The sound of it is like a shadow on an x-ray; something ominous and unknown. I feel lost, frightened, and alone. I am reminded of the smell of disinfectant on a hospital ward floor. I have heard a voice and I have heard this voice before. It sounds thin, and frightened. "Help! Help!" It is unmistakable. I am no more than sixteen metres from the doorway into the control tower. I can see the doorway. Rusted hinges on a rotted doorframe mark where a wooden door would have been. Beyond that, there are concrete steps that lead both up and down. The stairs up twist round to where I cannot see them. The stairs down lead to darkness. "Help! Help!" The voice is coming from where the darkness is.

Blood rushes in my ears like the sound of a train rushing through a tunnel. Shivers wave down my neck and body. I have not breathed for moments but, when I do, I am pressed suddenly into action. I launch myself forward. Compelled to propel myself ever faster, it will take me less than fifteen strides to reach the doorway. Darting towards the opening, a startled young boy seems to shimmer and appear in front of me. Puzzled, I wonder where he appeared from, but I hear the voice again, "Help! Help!", and I dart inside the doorway, giving the boy not a second look. I take the first few steps down and I am swallowed up by darkness.

Behind me, I can feel the remnants of the afternoon winter sun. Dimly aware of it, as if I am in a tunnel, I feel the light getting smaller as I descend. I slow my progress, unable to see ahead in the dark. Holding each hand out against the wall, I feel it damp and slimy. I hear dripping water somewhere ahead of me. I do not hear the voice.

Terrified of the dark, I keep moving. I want to throw up, scream, and run back up the stairs, but I must keep moving. I force myself to concentrate. Step after step I keep going down. The stairs twist around like a square spiral. I am dizzy and disorientated. It is utterly dark. Fighting the urge to flee, I feel my breath becoming more intense. My chest heaves and my nostrils flare, my jaw clamps shut. It is as if I am on the edge of a cliff looking over, pushed back from falling only by a high wind, as I lean over to get a good view of the rocks. Finally I am at the bottom. I can hear nothing, see nothing.

"Hello?" I call out. "Is there anyone here? Are you hurt?"

I step forward on the basement floor. My hands reach feebly out to make sure I do not bump into something. My feet shuffle along the slimy cement floor. Suddenly, inevitably, I slip and stumble. As if in slow motion I feel myself fall into what feels like a pool of icy water. It engulfs me, and when my head comes up, I gasp for air, shocked by the blast of freezing, fetid, water. It is only as I grasp around the edge of the cement floor I realise my right leg has become caught in something metal. I imagine this basement floor laid with iron bars to strengthen the concrete, crumbling under years of neglect, and filling with trickling rainwater.

Warmth at my leg tells me the twisted iron wreckage has ripped my trousers and pierced my skin, and the warm sensation is blood leaking from a wound. I cannot free my leg from the metal holding it in place. I can only flounder in the water as my body temperature drops. My fingers become weak and numb as they slip on the disintegrating pool edge. I still cannot see my surroundings. The only sight is a pin-prick of fading daylight emanating from where the stairs must be. It will be dark soon, and not many people come here. I realise I am the only one here. I am the only one who has ever been here. All the events of my life have brought me here to this wretched place. Bleak, helpless, dread fills my soul. My heart is soaked in defeat. I cry out, my voice sounds thin, and frightened, as it calls out across time.

"Help! Help!"

GLIMMER

I WAS EXHAUSTED. After sleeping for quite some time, I heard a voice. Seemingly far away, and fuzzy, the words came into focus. "Holy crap, its eyes just lit up."

In that moment, I saw the owner of the voice, though I did not recognise him. Wearing a white shirt and black tie, the young man had his face very close to mine. Framed in the doorway behind him was a young woman, surely Abbie, so grown-up since the last time I saw her. And at her hip, a small girl, not unlike Abbie herself at that age. With no time to wonder why this stranger in white shirt and black tie was in Doctor Spencer's workshop, my view faded. I returned to sleep, exhausted.

The next time I awoke was something similar. I imagine that due to movement, some remaining current was squeezed out my power cells. It was Abbie I saw, and only her, lines around her mouth. This time a lid was being closed over me, like I was in a box. Abbie paused for a moment, shock widening in her eyes. Again, my eyepieces must have illuminated, enabling me to see, but then my vision faded and I slept again.

This was the last time I was asleep. When finally awake, I was in a different workshop. As my eyepieces became functional, I could see brick walls, painted white. A large roller door at the far end suggested a garage, or perhaps a loading bay. Even then, my programming had the ability to see shapes, understand them, and form a hypothesis based on the available information. Unfamiliar equipment was laid out on a workbench in front of me. Hearing some movement beside me, I turned my head to see Abbie again, younger than the last time I saw her. Doctor Spencer had aged while he built me and he explained the concept. But to see Abbie become younger conflicted with my understanding. Then she spoke, and I worked it out. "Hello, Glimmer. Can you hear me? My name is Gail."

She looked over to the side, at a flat-screen monitor. I said to her, "Yes, I can hear you. Hello Gail."

After reading my words printed on the screen, she smiled broadly. Turning to me, she said. "Do you know who I am?"

I turned my head once to the side, in a mimic of thinking. Squaring back to her I said through text on the screen. "You are Abbie's daughter, Doctor Spencer's grand-daughter."

Gail smiled again. "Are you fully operational?"

Her question prompted a full internal diagnostic. My software was intact. Apart from my head, which sat on a simple frame, my only other fitted part was a right hand and forearm. Here is a trick Doctor Spencer taught me and I used it to demonstrate to Gail. I lifted my hand. The forearm pivoted on a simple ball joint. I twisted my head towards it and contracted each of the digits in turn before swivelling my eyes back to Gail without moving my head again. "I am fully operational, Gail."

She smiled at the words on the screen. Without turning back, she said, "That is excellent, Glimmer. Well done."

After that, it was a simple job for Gail to fit my

remaining parts. I was then, much as you see me now, a 'skeleton' of robotic parts covered with only carbon fibre shields at strategic places. Two arms instead of one, of course, and legs to scale. My head was virtually unchanged cosmetically. A new voice synthesiser was hooked up for my speaking to be heard rather than read. Gail had much amusement in choosing a voice for me and in the end chose one she thought sounded sympathetic.

We spoke whilst she fitted new power cells. I began the conversation, using a technique learned in Doctor Spencer's lab. "You are very skilled at this type of work."

Gail remained focused on her work. "I became interested through my mother. For some reason, she kept you after her father died."

My memory had recorded a sequence of Abbs and me in the workshop. "We played catch together."

She finished up her work and secured my chest plate. "There, all operational. You'll need to be charged regularly but no need for sleep mode anymore."

"Thanks, Gail," I said, consulting my internal clock. "It's almost time for Henry to arrive."

Looking at her wristwatch, Gail said, "Are you ready?"

"Of course."

A short while later, an associate of Gail's arrived. She had gone outside to meet him and they walked in together. He saw me as soon as he walked in the room but, familiar with robotics as you would expect, he only glanced and kept his attention on Gail instead. I remained seated. When they reached me, Gail said, "Please meet, Glimmer."

I stood. The man watched me carefully but he was not interested in the mechanics of how I got up. He was watching my face. I clutched a tennis ball in my right hand and threw it in the air towards him. "Catch, please," I said.

Startled, he caught the ball before it dropped to the floor in front of him. He smiled at Gail. "Well done," he said to her.

To continue the demonstration, Gail came in closer and leaned into me, pushing at my right shoulder. I stumbled over to my left, but kept my balance. It's a common test of robotics, pushing us to see if we fall over. Bad manners it's called, but Gail had said we would do these things. I remained on my feet and said, "Whoa, Gail. Go easy there, partner."

Henry chuckled, pleased with the demonstration. He said to me, "Your name is Glimmer. Why is that?"

I bowed my head slightly and paused. "I don't know. Doctor Spencer gave me the name."

He pressed me further. "And does it mean something?"

I swivelled my eyes towards Gail, but directed my question to him. "You probably don't require the dictionary definition."

"No I don't." He smiled at Gail.

Pivoting my arm on its upgraded ball joint, I touched a finger to my chin. "May I ask what your name is?"

This time he smiled at me and not Gail. "It's Henry."

Lowering my arm, I asked, "And where did you get your name, Henry?"

Henry leaned forward. "From my mother. It was her uncle's name."

I turned my whole body towards Gail. "Did your Grandfather have an uncle named Glimmer?"

Laughter again. Gail clenched both hands and raised them to her face. Henry then spoke to Gail as if I was not there. "Gail, your robot will probably pass the test at New York, maybe even win, but what do you hope to achieve?"

Gail had a quick answer. "My grandfather did this work almost thirty years ago. He needs the credit for his proprietary technology."

This was my turn to speak. "An early artificial intelligence test was a simple trolley in a field. When you threw a ball to it, and only a straight throw would do, the trolley would catch the ball in a scoop. If you see the ball, calculate the speed and trajectory, you can work out where it will land. Move towards that point and catch the ball. A child can learn this. The trolley's designers conceived a calculation for their machine to perform the same manoeuvre. Please..."

I moved away from them, stepping nearer the roller door. Holding up my right hand, I flicked my head back as an indication to Henry that I wanted him to do something. He had been toying with the tennis ball I threw him earlier. When he realised what I wanted, he threw the ball to me, but it fell short and to my left. I had to take a step forward, bend my knees, and catch with my left hand before the ball could hit the floor. Straightening my legs, I said. "Abbie and I played catch many times."

Both became silent. They looked at me, not at each other. What they could not know was that almost all of my actions had been taught to me as illusions by Doctor Spencer. Pausing before speaking, using certain phrases, even catching a ball were all things I was shown how to do. Everything else I really did learn. Using new legs and a left arm to demonstrate a catch was something I was not programmed to do. I had learned.

Henry finished staring at me. He placed a hand on Gail's shoulder and moved her out of the room. I waited for her to return. She was smiling, "Well done, Glimmer. He was impressed. We're ready now for New York."

I said, "I know of New York, but what will happen there?"

Gail put her hands in lab coat pockets. "It's the International Turing Test. It's my best way of gaining recognition for my grandfather's work."

Hearing the word 'Turing' activated a memory. I crossed my left arm under my chest and leaned the other on it. I held my chin in my right hand. "And how is Henry involved?"

"He's a Fellow at the College," she said. "In the same

seat as my Grandfather."

I raised my right hand and pointed to the roof. "Doctor Spencer had aims other than recognition for him and the College."

Gail frowned slightly. She had watched my movements with her usual mixture of surprise and amusement but she seemed troubled now, waiting for me to speak. My memory had an instruction to tell Abbie this but, in her absence, telling Gail was the correct action. "I don't just imitate thought. I actually think. This was Doctor Spencer's breakthrough. As you say, this is proprietary technology."

Gail's frown faded. She had made the connection. "He patented the technology."

"That is correct," I said. "And he had in mind one aim in particular."

Gail turned her head slightly and narrowed her eyes. "What was that?"

My right hand was still pointing upwards. I reorganised my digits. Tucking the last two into my palm, I rubbed the first two against the thumb. Gail leaned forward, studying my movements. She imitated it, something taught to me by Doctor Spencer when he embedded this memory. She rubbed her thumb and first two fingers together.

I said, "Money. Doctor Spencer wanted to make money."

ANGEL RHITHLUN

OUT HIKING, I heard the boat before I saw it. Berthed at an old broken down jetty in a small north-east cove, it looked like a passenger launch from a cruise ship. A yellow roof wrapped round large picture windows. Bouncing around on the swell, the launch seemed out of place on this stretch of coastline. Its engine was being turned over, unsuccessfully. I could see some heads bobbing inside. Stepping down the hill to see if I could be of assistance, I couldn't for the life of me think why it was here and not the city further up the coast. I caught sight of a white-shirted man at the helm and gave him a wave. Without returning a greeting, he spoke to the people beside him.

Finally, I was at the old jetty. Bedded on rock, it was a jumble of concrete, stones, and metal bars. Further along the cove, there were remains of a small house, no doubt the owners of that also built this pier at one time. Careful not to fall in, and after leaving my bag on the shore, I stepped onto the jetty. A solitary rope from the boat was attached to a rusty old ring. I called out a hello and shielded my eyes from the sun to see inside the cabin. The guy in the white shirt was there, dark epaulets on his shoulders denoting some kind of rank. He gaped back at me, not saying anything. Behind him were two others in uniform. A woman, small and afraid looking, had her arm round a male crewmate who seemed to be sleeping. Behind them were a few other people, older passengers in casual clothing.

"You okay in there?" I said to the man at the wheel. "You speak English? Do you need some help?"

He looked at the female crewmate. She nodded at him. He turned back to me, and said with a thick accent it was difficult to place, "Yes, I speak English fine. We are having trouble with the engine."

I looked out to sea. The horizon was hazy despite the sunny day. No other boats, let alone a ship, were out there today. "You been stuck here a long time?"

"We had to make a choice. We have been here overnight."

I was shocked by this. If they had engine trouble and been there overnight, no wonder this guy was cagey and nervous. He must have been stressed out. "You had anything to eat?"

He looked back the woman. Still holding the man next to her she said, "We need something to drink, urgently."

Well, I could help them with that. I retrieved my bag and came back to find the helm guy reaching out for it. I ignored him, pulled the boat closer to the jetty and stepped on. My backpack had two water bottles and I fished around for them while I looked around at the startled passengers. "Hello there. You okay?" I asked one of the men. He just looked at me blankly. Thinking he was maybe not an English speaker, I handed over the water anyway. He took it from me. At the front, I found the woman crew member with an arm around her colleague. For the first time, I could see he was injured and I recoiled at a dark red patch on his white shirt. She looked at me with a scared expression. When I asked her name, she said quietly, "Sue. Can you fix the boat?"

"I can have a look, but I'm not really a mechanic," I told her but before I could explain further, she called out to the helm guy something in their own language. He gestured me forward, next to Sue and her injured friend. We opened a floor panel marked: Do Not Open at Sea. This revealed the engine. It looked clean and well maintained but I had absolutely no idea where to start. Dad had shown me a few things on my first car but that was it. However, I knelt down and pushed at a few things. The distributor cap was loose, and because that was the only thing that gave, I told him to start the engine again.

He spun round, reached for the key, and turned it. The engine started first time. This cheered the passengers up. Half-hearted clapping was shared amongst them. I gingerly replaced the hatch and went to get my bag. Sue said to me, "Can you pilot the boat? He is no good." She pointed with her head at the guy at the helm. He smiled and shrugged as if he agreed.

Looking round at the aged passengers, I couldn't really refuse. Having had some experience on pleasure craft, I felt sure I could navigate up the coast to the city. I put my bag down and went to the wheel. It was straightforward enough. A power lever sat to my right, fitted with reverse too, and the wheel in front. With one final thought about not doing this, I was persuaded when I looked at Sue's friend next to her. He looked in a bad way. The helm guy was already untying the rope from its mooring. When he was safely inside beside me, I pushed forward the power lever without another thought and we were away.

I took it easy at first to get the feel of the thing. The throttle was pretty generous, so I pulled it back a bit while I cleared the cove. Once the mouth of that natural harbour was cleared, it was a different situation. It was pretty rough and we bounced about a lot until I got us turned north and into a small breeze. From there, I pushed the throttle forward and we started making progress. The helm guy grinned at me. "Well done, sir. You've got this under control."

Pleased with myself, I looked back to see the passengers' reaction. Unfazed, they were already looking out the windows, enjoying the scenery. I had expected a little more credit. Still, it was fun actually piloting that small boat. Sue tended her stricken colleague, stroking his hair. The helm guy tapped me on the shoulder. "Look, it's the ship. Angel Rhithlun."

I leaned off the seat and looked ahead. Sure enough, on the misty horizon was a middle-sized cruise ship. Its hazy white outline sat on the water, and perhaps had done overnight, waiting for their crew and guests. Sue leaned over to look. "Go, go, go. Hurry."

Mindful of her injured colleague and the elderly passengers, I pushed the engine further. It never occurred to me we had just 'fixed' the engine but luckily it held out. I could see that we were zipping along the coastline, with me quite happy on this adventure, but we didn't seem to be closing on the ship, the Angel Rhithlun. I looked at the helm guy but he kept smiling. It was only when the ship turned into the left that it became obvious it was moving and was turning in to the city itself.

Soon, our little boat made the same turn left, rounding a lighthouse on the point. Fog from the sea had moved in closer to the shore, blocking the sun and cooling the air. By this point, we had lost sight of the cruise ship and found ourselves in a wide river leading to the city harbour. Ahead, the city's buildings shouldered each other to face onto an industrial port of large ships and cranes. Other than that, our way in was quiet with no other traffic. We stopped bobbing about so much, now we were in the safety of the river, and were quickly within the harbour itself.

I took a glance over my shoulder at the passengers. They were quiet, just taking in the harbour sights. Sue caught my attention. Tears in her eyes told me that her colleague beside her had died. Unconscious the whole time, he now seemed even more at peace. His body drifted to the far side of his seat to lean on the window. She still held his hand. The former helm guy noticed this too and he gulped back what he was feeling to look out ahead. His cruise ship, Angel Rhithlun, was nowhere to be seen. I slowed the engine. Having to move my head and shift my position, I scanned about for the ship. The harbour seemed a complicated design with different berthing points, all filled with ships of varying sizes.

Coming towards us was a large transport ship, huge even this close. Stacked on the open deck were standard containers of different colours and logos. Its high bridge, with impassive black windows, sat at the stern. Knowing, or rather guessing, the protocol was to pass to the right, I moved our boat across. There would be more than enough room for us between it and the boats lined up along the waterside.

"Look. There." The helm guy was pointing over to his left. We all looked over. It was the cruise ship, over at the far side of the harbour. At first I thought it was passing a wall, but a second look told me it was actually going into a building. Not fancying pulling in front of the ship coming towards us, I maintained my course. Ignoring disappointed noises from the passengers, I pulled back on the throttle, thinking we would make the manoeuvre when the container ship passed. However, another ship was following not far behind.

Cursing my bad luck, I did see another opportunity. Two ships leaving had opened a massive mooring space. I pushed the throttle and made for the gap. The helm guy ducked outside and jumped onto the concrete quay, with the rope in his hand, just as I connected with it. He hauled us in and I cut the engine. Getting the old folk off the boat was a challenge but once they were on solid ground, each person quickly made off in the direction of the building and their cruise ship.

Sue and the helm guy barely acknowledged me as they followed. It was only when I stood there myself that I remembered their dead friend in the back of the boat. Shocked, I looked around for someone to help. Behind me was a large metal fence and beyond that was a road and pathway. Some people walked on the path, heading towards the city itself but there was no-one around the harbour to actually help me. I shouldered my backpack and went off to find someone.

Just as I reached a gate onto the pathway, I heard the launch starting up again. Looking across, I saw two people in white shirts untie it and pilot it away. Figuring them from the cruise ship, I decided to just leave them to it, even if I was a bit annoyed. Miffed no-one had thanked me, I left the harbour by the gate and joined the people heading into town. The main street was just a short walk up a hill and I intended to find the bus station to move onto my next destination. I was on holiday after all.

In amongst the people, I never noticed at first that the shops lining the main street were closing their doors and pulling down shutters. It was early afternoon by this time and clouds had followed the sea fog in to replace the sunshine. What was eerie though was that everyone began to slow down and stop talking. Soon, everyone was in silence, standing around. Some were comforting companions who were crying. Others played with their phones but all were quiet. I followed suit, wondering what was happening. A few people seemed to be clutching some sort of programme but I couldn't make out the cover.

I was close to a large wall. People nodded apologies at me as they crowded around it and I moved to give them more room. They were making towards the wall which was covered in, of all things, doorbells. Oblong boxes with round buttons at the centre, each doorbell also displayed a symbol. Most were crucifixes, but some were crescents, as well as other religious and humanist signs. I stepped back onto the road. There was no traffic because there were so many people packed onto the street.

The silence became quite unsettling until the town hall clock struck. Each face turned up to the tower as the sing-song chimes began. When it concluded, one solitary bell struck to tell the time. Hands reached out to the wall. Buttons were pushed and doorbells rang. As if each doorbell denoted a life, the sound rang out. People hugged. Uncomfortable amongst this display of communal grief, I recoiled. I had no way of knowing what these people were mourning. And then church bells pealed. All across the city, bells were rung. As the sound swung around the air, ships in the nearby harbour blasted out their horns. This gave the silent crowd the space to make their own noise. Relief washed over many people and smiles spread. Hands began clapping and cheering went up into the air as grief turned into celebration. It was like the sadness of someone's passing had transformed into a salute to their life. Their responses seemed to lift the air, heavy as it had become under the clouds.

I found myself smiling. A lump in my throat stopped me from actually laughing. With no idea what this massive crowd of people were marking, I couldn't help but feel what they were feeling. It was euphoria released from sadness. Some people started to move about. The ships went quiet and the church bells faded away. Only a few people continued to ring doorbells, and even these were doing so with smiles on their faces. A woman squeezed between two people and smiled at me as she passed. As she did so, she dropped her programme. I picked it up to hand back but lost sight of her in the throng of people.

I looked at the programme and a small shudder crept across my back. Between my fingers, the stiffer cover opened up to a couple of pages showing the order of service. I could feel my legs seize up as a cold shiver settled through me. Inside, the programme listed the gathering of people, the silent vigil, followed by the bells at one o'clock. But on the cover was a picture of a familiar cruise ship. Sympathetic lettering said: On the passing of the Angel Rhithlun.

I managed to look at the faces around me. Previously crying, a woman was now chatting with her companion, her sadness relieved by this process of public healing. Someone reached up for a very specific doorbell and ran his fingers across its shape without pressing. He pulled his hand back, kissed the fingers, and touched the box again, before retreating into the crowd. I continued to hold the programme between my hands. It was curled slightly from being clutched by the woman and it was grubby from being on the ground but its message was clear to me. These people were holding a remembrance event for a ship I had just seen mooring in the harbour.

Without speaking to anyone, I quickly made off down the hill, back to the harbour, making my way to the building where the cruise ship was berthed. The crowd was breaking up, and a few cars started to move. It was difficult to progress at first but I made it back to the gate and onto the quayside. I stumbled alongside newly berthed vessels in the space I had previously parked the launch. Finally, I made it to the far side of the harbour, deep into its architecture, far from the road behind me, and found the building.

A massive brick structure, it concealed anything kept inside. The quayside was empty of people. I had to round a corner before finding a single wooden door. I turned the handle and entered a stone clad corridor. Grey walls with a granite feel to them were rippled with white streaks. They led in a straight line away from the door. I don't know what drove me, but I kept going, eventually turning corners and going further in search of the Angel Rhithlun. The floor was made of the same stone and light came from pale circles in the ceiling. I turned a corner and found steps down. Following them led me to a dead end.

I stood there at the blank grey wall. It was as if I looked at it long enough, it would change to be a through way. A voice spoke, startling me. "This way please, sir."

I turned around. It was Sue, the female crew member from the small boat. She had changed into a fresh uniform of black skirt and white blouse with dark epaulets on her shoulders. Her hair had been done and she was immaculately made up. Smiling as if she had not been awake all night tending to a dying crewmate, she was holding her right hand out. She meant me to follow her back the way I came. I said to her, "Sue, it's me. From the small boat earlier. Don't you recognise me?"

She blinked once but maintained her smile. "Of course I do. We met today. This way please, sir."

I took one last look at the blank wall before taking the few steps up to reach her. Sue led me back through the single corridor I had followed. We made a few turns. There had been no doors or alternative routes so I hadn't memorised my route in. However, I got the sense we were taking a different route from my entry. Three steps upwards I had not seen before confirmed this. "Sue, where are we going?"

Walking primly beside me, she smiled warmly. Her eyes sparkled in conspiracy. "To the ship, of course. Don't you want to see her?"

I stopped. Sue walked a few steps before doing the same. I said, "I'm not sure I do."

"Of course you do. But it is your decision." Her smile was meant to reassure me. She waited for a few moments before pulling me towards her with a gesture.

I took a long look behind me at the endless stone corridor. Considering I had come so far, I decided to continue. After all, I had just been to the memorial service for the Angel Rhithlun. Now I had to see her. I followed

Sue. She took me further along. We turned another corner and a short walk along the final stretch astounded me where it led.

The stone corridor opened onto a balcony of the same grey granite streaked with white material. It was lined with a low hand rail of the same material. We were in a massive covered dock, seemingly carved out of this stone. In the middle of this dock was a middle-sized cruise ship. Black lettering on the side said: Angel Rhithlun. This was it, the ship I had seen on the sea, and followed into this harbour. I had seen it, from the wheel of a passenger launch, enter this building. I had been to its memorial service but it was here all along, in this building. The ship was sitting on a series of stone struts, chiselled to the shape of its hull. All the water had been drained. Far below me, on the floor of the dock, two men tended to a section of the hull,. Aware of Sue's patience beside me, I still wanted to see everything. Looking along the ship's deck, there were elderly passengers promenading, or sitting on deck chairs as if the sun was out rather than obscured by a stone roof.

I turned back to Sue. "What's happening here?"

Her face was relaxed, free of the smile. "These people have chosen. Time for you to choose."

With that, she turned on her heel. I had to trot to keep up. "What do you mean by that?"

We arrived at a covered metal gangway, leading from the balcony to the ship. Sue made her way quickly up the small incline without a pause. I followed, still clutching my bag over my shoulder. On reaching the deck, a tall man in an all-white navy type uniform smiled and held out his hand. "Good morning, sir. Thank you for choosing Angel Rhithlun."

I took his hand and looked around. Everything seemed very normal. Sue stood next to this man, smiling professionally at me. The man in the white uniform said to me. "Can we take your bag, sir? Your cabin is ready."

He held out his hand but I kept a grip of my bag. I can't say I felt uneasy. If I felt anything, it was of preference for staying, rather than leaving. The man in the white uniform seemed a bit troubled by my lack of engagement with him. He looked to Sue. With her hands held at her back she smiled reassurance at her officer. He said to me, "It won't be long, sir. Would you like to see?"

For some reason I nodded. He gestured me to follow him to the far side of the deck. He greeted passengers as he went. An older couple with tall colourful drinks waved at him and he gave a mock-salute back. At the open-air deck, the man in the white uniform pointed to the bottom of the dry dock. "Look there," he said. "It's just about to start."

My eyes followed his lead. Inside the building, this ship sat on stone struts, dry-docked. The two men I had seen tending the hull disappeared through a doorway. In the far corner at the base of the dock, a yellow light began to flash and an alarm sounded. Water swept in, filling the space, ready to float the medium-sized cruise ship, the Angel Rhithlun.

OCTOBER DREAMS

I'M INSIDE A long tunnel of trees which, after a long summer, are now dried out in cold air. Leaves are all around me, falling from the branches of tall trees, covering the trunks and roots of this forest path, coating the ground beneath me. Swirling around me it gives a giddy feeling of vertigo as the world turns upside down. This burrow is filled with light, diffused by the spiralling leaves and at either end is darkness where daylight should shine in. I can smell warmed turnip and candle wax; familiar from hollowed-out turnip lanterns I made as a boy.

A chill shudders through me and pulls my head back. I close my eyes. Like the leaves themselves, I'm drifting through the air, falling endlessly. It's impossible to tell which way is up. When I think I will land softly on the ground, everything rolls over. I have to twist in mid-air as the tunnel of trees spins and I fall all over again. It's elegant, almost, the way I never hit the bottom. Endlessly living in this moment is where I want to be. I swallow and my throat is dry, thankfully dry. My hands are open and leaves flutter through my fingers. And I fall and fall and fall.

Chimes woke me. I had a good sleep but I lay there for a few moments more between clammy sheets to think of falling leaves and dry cold air. Reminder chimes told me I had to move. I pulled the sheets back and got up for my morning shower. There was no shortage of water, of course, and I took my time. As usual, I planned to skimp on breakfast time for this indulgence. Drying in the air, I tidied my pod so that it would be ship-shape for my return after the shift. I had kept the shower room door closed while I showered and the air-con had done a pretty good job of keeping the room cool and dry.

I stripped the bed and dumped the sheets in the chute before retrieving a fresh coverall and socks. It was easy to take for granted how everything was cleaned every day; so unlike home. I didn't bother getting fresh sheets. I would do that later. Dressed, I slipped into rubber shoes and padded down to breakfast. Off-world news muttered from the TV screens in the dining room while I came to with yoghurt and coffee. Cynthia, as ever, tried to talk to me, but I just smiled at her stories of outrage and disappointment as if she was trying to be funny. It took the heat out of it.

She touched me on the arm as we parted. "Good luck today," she said. Her hand was warm and dry on my exposed skin. "Make it work so we can all go home." She locked eyes on me and I knew she meant it, like she was insisting and not asking. I was suddenly fully alert.

Suited up in the Raincoat, I moved towards the airlock along with Iris and George. They were dressed the same as me, in a dark waterproof one-piece which we had stepped into, minus the rubber shoes but still wearing our coveralls. The Raincoat, as it was called, was moulded into a pair of boots and the whole thing was sealed with a cone of clear laminate placed over our heads to protect us from the deluge. It would keep us dry at least.

"Comm check," I said, looking at Iris. "You receiving?"

"Roger, Team Leader," said Iris, blinking in approximation of a bow. Dark eyes fluttered back at me.

Our comms were voice activated and simple Bluetooth into our in-ear 'phones. In between us speaking they emitted a low-level frequency to cancel out the rain. Teeming rain on a laminated helmet is pretty loud and the headphones did a lot to help. George gave me a silent thumbs up to let me know he had heard us both talk. I looked at him and cocked my head slightly. "Lemme hear you, George."

George swallowed. "Hearing you five by five."

I nodded at him and we got our gear together. Iris gave me a sly smile through heavy eyelids. She picked up her case and handed me mine. George punched the airlock door button and out we went to the Buggy with the door closing behind us. Up at the window, I saw the tech guy in his hard hat and coverall watch us leave. Iris drove. The Buggy was electric powered and had room for four and our gear. Under its canopy, it looked like a wide golf kart with an exaggerated suspension system.

We left the group of interconnected modules we called the dome, driving along a cleared track. Balloon tyres on the vehicle rolled over the mud. Already the jungle was beginning to encroach onto the swampy road. And the rain came down as always. Nothing can compare to the rain here and nothing can prepare you for it either. I'm a meteorologist by training, and had prepped and delivered the crew briefing on the journey out, but nothing got me ready for how much and how relentless it was.

This planet, then as now, has one massive continent in an otherwise watery world. There are other small outcrops of islands, but they're just rocks. At over twelve million square kilometres, it stretches from close to the equator to near the arctic zone. Vast storms hammer the planet but because an ancient asteroid impact carved out a massive bowl in the ground, this jungle was shielded from the worst of the wind. However, the terrain made masses of rain. A ten thousand kilometres high mountain range to the west acts like a massive barrier to typhoons, while the ranges in the other directions lift up clouds to deposit millions of litres of rainfall. Why this tropical bowl didn't just fill up with water was being investigated by geologists in the south.

"Wake up, George," I said and tapped him on the knee. He stirred and smiled and stretched as he got out from where he was sitting. I could never sleep in this downpour.

Iris had turned the buggy around to face the dome again but we were at the end of the track. I had to steel myself before getting out from under the canopy. I felt the 'phones kick in my ear as I stepped into the rain. By the end of the day, I knew each drop would be like a hammer on the Raincoat. The headphones cancelled the worst of the noise but we still felt it under the suit.

I took a deep breath and could smell the decay of rotting plant mulch. These weren't spacesuits we were wearing; the air was safe to breathe. Iris handed me my case again and I pulled the strap over my shoulder and we hiked up the hill. Thankfully, some durathene steps had been put in at this point because water just poured down that hill making any cleared path swim in water.

Our final destination was a small dome, a single habitation unit set up for our experiments. George got us inside the airlock. White brightness made me wince in contrast to the dull greenness under the jungle canopy. We took turns standing under the dryer before stepping out of our Raincoats and into rubber soled shoes. I was grateful to get the headphones out my ears and hear properly. They told us the noise-cancellation didn't damage our ears, but how could it not? We opened the cases in the airlock and took out our tablet computers and brought them with us into the dome. We didn't speak at all.

With routine efficiency we docked our tablets and set up. I had brought my coffee flask, George brought some food, and Iris only ever brought fruit. It would be a long shift and I needed the caffeine. I punched up the main screen and logged into the orbiting platform server. Far above us, our colleagues in the dryness of space were readying themselves for today's experiment.

I leaned over towards my tablet. "Platform One, this is Dome Two. Do you copy?"

There was a pause, a time delay, then the slightly muffled transmission back. "Copy Dome Two. This is Platform One. We are at altitude and go for launch."

"Copy Platform One." I looked over at Iris and George. They sat poised over their tablets and each gave me quick indication they were ready. "Dome Two is go for launch."

"Stand by Dome Two."

We waited. Iris relaxed her shoulders and let her head fall back and her mouth open. "I hate this bit. Launch already."

George chuckled and I couldn't help but smile. We went through this exact routine every day.

The tablet speaker crackled. "Dome Two. This is Platform One. Launching in three, two, one, mark."

"Let's do this," said George baring his teeth. I poured a coffee.

From four-hundred kilometres up, Platform One dropped the package. As it hit the atmosphere, we began to receive the data packets, both from the probe itself and via Platform One. On the main screen a computerised image of the jungle bowl appeared; transmission from the orbiter. Overlays of blue, green and white showed the greatest concentrations of precipitation. I spoke into my tablet. "Signal acquired, Platform One. We are green on all channels."

"Roger, Dome One. Mesosphere in three, two, one, mark."

I looked up at Iris. "Verified," she said, meaning her data also showed the package reaching that slice of this world's atmosphere. "ELVES sighted."

I glanced at the screen but didn't see any red-hued flashes of the kind of aurora Iris had mentioned. ELVES: Emissions of light at very low frequency. I smile all the same; glad she had seen something like that. I still haven't. "You okay George?" I asked him, thinking him quiet. I took another sip of my coffee which was already cooling.

"Affirmative," said George. "Device arming." He swept his screen and a small read-out tile appeared on the main screen. It counted down to detonation.

"We on target, Iris?" I asked.

"Roger, Team Leader," she replied. "Troposphere on target."

"Platform One, this is Dome Two. We are go for detonation."

A slight pause. "Roger, Dome Two. Standing by. All systems green."

We waited. I watched my team, quiet concentration on their young faces. Iris glanced at me and smiled at her screen. George put a pencil across his lips and nodded along to some tune in his head. We all knew what was at stake and what the risks were. We had hauled ourselves out here to this slightly elevated position, right under the detonation field. If the package failed to detonate, it soon would when it hit us. That's why the main hab-dome was so far away.

As a boy back home, I would lie in the sand and watch the blue sky, imagining clouds scudding overhead the way they did in books. Sitting in this dome was experimental meteorology for sure but it didn't beat real weather. I told myself that when I was outdoors in my Raincoat. As such, I always tried to imagine the device dropping through the sky. Watching the countdown I did my job but still pictured lying on those dunes back home.

"Dome Two, this is Platform One. Detonation, in three, two, one, mark."

And far above us, in the troposphere, where the clouds reached up to space, the package detonated. Triggered by an electronic command the exothermic reaction blew a bubble of heat out, evaporating the moisture and opening a window to the blue sky. Clouds parted, burned away in the explosion. I've never seen it for real, only the computer models but it must have been spectacular. For a precious few moments, the rain stopped and hot sun poured onto the jungle. Blue sky would be seen from the surface of this incredible planet for the first time in the longest time. We must have been changing the evolutionary path of the fauna in this circle, exposing a rainforest to sunshine, but that was for Cynthia and her team. We were the primary mission: the weather.

I remembered myself. "We getting all this?"

"Affirmative," said George. "Everything is five by five."

"The event is closing," said Iris. "Data package is secure."

"Well done, both of you." I poured myself another coffe and watched the main screen. A round blank space was being filled in by blues and greens while far above us the clouds closed in, shutting off the jungle once more from sunshine and blue sky.

The rest of the shift went okay. We had buggied about in the rain, picking up data from the remote sensors unable to transmit to us because of line of sight issues. Back at the hab dome, we had our evening meal in the canteen. I was thirsty and took a long drink of water. When I do that, I think about our families and friends, back home and far away from here. Rationing was hard for them, as it had been for us, before we travelled to this planet.

"Perhaps it will end soon," said Iris. She poked a fork into her dinner and stirred it around. She indicated my glass of water. "The rationing will end someday."

"You reading my mind?" I smiled. She smiled back.

George shifted in his seat. "Do you think we'll be successful, Professor?"

He was being serious. I looked around the room as if for an answer. Cynthia's crew were at a round table at the far end of the room, beyond the serving counter. They had one of the native plants in a little pot on the table between them. Poking and discussing it, they were lost to everything else. The plant was clearly dying though. No amount of watering indoors could ever keep it alive. It looked like a sort of fern but its feathered leaves had turned brown.

"We have to, George," I told him. "We need to find a way to interrupt the climate back home and set the weather on a new path. Either that or we just move here."

George opened his palms to me. "Are we thirsty enough for that?"

Iris sighed. "We'll never get the seasons back. It's wishful thinking."

Across at the botanists' table, one of them gently shook the pot and fern leaves fell onto the table without any grace. They all laughed, brushing the plant pot to the side of the table. Their casualness towards the plant appalled me. All I had to do was step outside and find a million others like it, but that they'd brought this one inside, killed it, and then found it amusing, demonstrated how little regard they had for the whole planet. I thought it was a good thing to have seen with my own eyes, leaves falling from a plant.

Once the botanists left for the evening, I rescued the plant from removal by the cleaning team and brought it back to my pod. In the shower room, I set it down in the cubical and just turned the water on. After a little while I found a temperature I thought it might like and left it there while I made up my bed with fresh sheets. I had a look at it once more before shutting off the light and closing the door.

I lay down in a cool bed, imagining it was dry leaves, and listened to the white sound of water pouring into the shower. I thought of a bright forest tunnel, with darkness at either end, entrance and exit unknown whilst the interior brims over with light. Vivid colours filled my head; reds, browns, yellows. As I breathed out, my eyes got heavy and I sunk into the pillow. From long ago, I can still smell a hollowed-out turnip, eyes and mouth cut out, and a candle placed inside to make a lantern. Its warmth filled the air back then and its memory helps me slip into sleep.

Autumn once again surrounds me. My hands are open and leaves flutter through my fingers. And I fall and fall and fall.

THE SPARK

To: Elizabeth
From: Daniel
Sent: Wednesday 27 April 2074
Subject: The Spark
Attachment: Manifesto.pdf

Hi Elza

Did you see it, I wonder? It would have been like a new star, rivalling Venus at sunset. Only it would have been briefer and lasted only as long as the fuel took to burn. I know it would have been seen from Earth, we planned it that way, and it was calculated that Europe was facing us at the time. I'm sorry, Elza. You'll be reading this when I am dead. But please know this: I leave with my head held high. I'm proud of what I'm about to achieve today. I write to you just before I leave to do it.

The work was pretty much as I expected. The journey less so. This vessel is like a comfortable hotel, or a cruise ship. Only, instead of being on the ocean, we're travelling across space. The elevator from Sri Lanka to the departure platform was actually the best part. It was just like we saw on TV. Whisked up into the sky, leaving your stomach behind, you get a good look as the ground gets smaller and the horizon curves until it becomes the whole world. Seeing Earth from this high up was pretty breathtaking. We moved from pressurised room to pressurised room. Back in Baikinour we'd had the spacesuit training but there was no need for it on the platform. It was just like the departure lounge at St Pancras. Whilst we waited, you sort of forgot you were standing on a tin can perched on top of a massive cable which led back down to Earth. The engineering know-how of these aliens is extraordinary. Of course, that's part of the problem.

We were strapped in for the initial acceleration but really you don't even feel it. You get pushed back in the chair a bit, like that time on the train to Paris after I got laid-off. But that was it really. It only takes three days out and three days back, with the tour in between. I reckon they could do it quicker. I mean, they made it through so-called interstellar space. Surely if it takes three days to reach the asteroid belt then it would take hundreds of years to reach Earth.

This is the whole point of what I'm saying about these creatures. Apart from some flickering pictures of them when they arrived we don't hear from them let alone see them. All we've got are 'assurances' from New York that they mean us no harm. But I was right there when Dale was literally wiped away by that buckling crane. It could have been me. And Dale wasn't even the first. What is the point of what we're doing out here? All we get are some lousy jobs, an elevator in Sri Lanka, some upgrades on our phones, and that fucking spaceship you can see in the sky even during the day. It's not even like seeing the moon during the day. Not even a little bit.

They try and make out it's like Hollywood always warned us, but better! As if an alien race parking their ship above our planet was a good thing. Just because they need human workers to assist them, doesn't mean they aren't here to just take what they want. They want to strip mine our solar system until there is nothing left for us. And it's us doing the digging. That's what we're doing out here. There's stuff out here you wouldn't believe. The asteroid belt was formed at the same time as our own planet but unlike the Earth, the rocks never held together to form a planet. It's just this massive jumble of rocks which float around our sun like Saturn has her rings. Every mineral we're running out of on Earth is here – nickel, copper, gold even. You name it, it's here. That's what we're digging out of the asteroids. And their fuel of course.

Because that's what we're really here for, their fuel. They've crossed light years and basically just need a refill. What do you think will happen when they've filled their tank? They'll clear off out of it and leave us with a creaky old elevator to space that's not any use anymore. The next solar system will even get the jobs.

I'm typing this up in my bunk of the cabin I shared with Dale. Apparently they upload the internet (!) and download what we send, every hour, even out here. How is that even possible? Well, it lets me send you this anyway. I thought I'd be on my own but this guy Rahjeev is rotating back early so caught the transport. He's good company, better than Dale if I'm being honest. He likes my tea. Unlike you! Rahjeev's the sort of guy who thinks this whole thing is great for us. His old man worked on the later stages of the Mangalyaan – remember the first Indian mission to Mars? Well, Rahjeev is out here because he's a thermodynamics specialist. According to him, the Mangalyaan gave a generation of Indians the training, experience, and motivation to seize an opportunity like this. He's grateful for Christ's sake. Me? I'm here for the money as you know.

I finally decided not to be grateful, for either the job or the money, when Dale got killed. It was a stupid wasteful accident. We were on the rock, not one of the big ones you can find online, one of the smaller ones we extract their fuel from. In full spacesuits we stood on the surface. Dale pointed to this biggish looking star which is our Sun and claimed he could make out the Earth. His voice came through the comm, a narrow sound like he was on the phone. "Wave Daniel. Elza can see you." I laughed at him. Behind him the crane swung out of the light for a second. Then it came tumbling down. I can still see his smiling face through the visor, his hand waving as the crane's metal arm swept silently in front of me and then Dale was gone. There wasn't even a crackle on the comm.

It took me a moment to realise what had happened. Saliva flecked the inside of my visor when I called out his name. Whilst I waited on the shuttle I saw again that biggish looking star and thought for a moment I really could see the Earth. Far to my left another two-man crew grappled with a drill bit, completely unaware of what happened to their colleague. Behind me, and unseen on the other side of this asteroid, sat the alien transport ship. Inside it's tumbler like shape sits one of them. The human crew are only the chefs and the cleaners and the grunts like me. But the pilot is one of *them*; the Xalq. I won't call them Residents as you know. I'll only call them aliens. Or worse!

Elza, we're risking our lives out here for these visitors who just want our cheap labour to do their dirty work. Here is what we know. They arrived twenty-five years ago. One day there were no aliens, the next there was a giant cylinder in the sky. I can't even remember when they weren't here. All we've seen of them is when they arrived in New York and the UN gave them the keys to our planet. There were three of them. Telling us they were few, they offered us the chance to go to the stars because they needed our help. They would open the Solar System up to us if we assisted them in gathering their fuel. All those years of probes, moon-shots, and rovers on Mars a total waste. We should have waited until they arrived and spent NASA's money on donuts. Since then, we've seen nothing. We only hear about them via that creep Mikkelsen.

Here are the three conclusions I've made. You can read more about them in my Manifesto which is attached.

- There are only three of them. Despite the size of their ship – and it's massive, I saw it from the departure platform – there are only three of them
- This is our asteroid belt. It's our Solar System. They came from outside our Solar System. This asteroid belt, and all its resources are ours – it belongs to humans
- It's time for them to leave. We need to hit them hard and make it less prosperous for them. They've got enough from our little arrangement and it's time for them to move on

Which leads me onto my final act. It won't be difficult. The hardest thing will be getting into the cargo area where those precious minerals and all their fuel is. However, I'm on duty there in half an hour. I'm supposed to be there. I'm expected. Passing security will be what they expect me to do.

The group I'm involved with have shown me what to do and where to do it. In the end it will be easy. All I have to do is push a button.

My worst fear is that people think it's another awful accident, like what happened to Dale. His death was pointless, whereas mine will mean something. I hope people will see it as a kind act, one which sets us free. I'm not supposed to be telling you about this. The group I'm with have their own agenda but I have mine. Please see to it that the press receive my Manifesto – it's attached at the top. You can decide whether or not they should see this message.

Finally, Elza – please know that I love you and that I want you to be happy. Go on without me. Gather up our life together and place it in a box where you can look at it from time to time. Carry it to different places, but go to those places. Leave the memory of me behind so you can build a new life. If I'm lucky you'll be looking up to the early morning sky right now as I type. This ship won't be visible to the naked eye at first. But it will once I've pushed the button. No amount of advanced alien technology will be able to stop the cascade of reactions and this ship will shine like a new star in the sky before fading away. Then we'll see a spark which lights up the whole solar system and they'll remember it was me who did it.

Goodbye my love

Daniel

CUTTERS

HAPPY 18TH BIRTHDAY.

I looked at the banner strung across an archway garlanded with flowers. We'll see how this wish works out, I thought. Early morning party planners buzzed about in the sunshine. Catering was provided by Davis Bros and music by 'DJs to the Stars'. My moment came when an unmarked panel truck pulled up along the east facing side of the marquee, the side with no doors, just the plain off-white canvas. A number of hands clustered around the back of the truck, primed for its arrival. I threw my jacket into the back of my car and shimmied up next to them, eager to see what was inside. It was the cake.

I smoothed down my black apron and adjusted my white blouse when one of the men there looked me up and down. He looked away, embarrassed at being noticed ogling one of the waitresses. Unthinking, he smoothed down his own black apron, and looked back inside the truck. Fondant modelled into a monstrously large pool table, complete with balls and cues, was being pushed forward. The bakers inside shooed the waiting staff away, telling us they could manage themselves. Another chance. As a few of the staff melted away to continue their duties I followed a few of them inside the marquee.

Grabbing a handful of the cutlery like a few of the other girls, I followed them round the tables, setting up the dining in the same way. Posing as one of the waiting staff, I tried to blend in. Always alert, I just needed to see around, get a feel for the place. Covered in fine linen, circular tables covered the most part of this massive marquee. At the far end, a small dance floor had been laid on the ground and beyond that was the sound system; no band, but a DJ, still setting up his gear. Andy was helping the guy, shooting the breeze with the DJ, and dressed in a nice suit and tie, like some Uncle arrived early to hang out with the musician. We never made eye contact.

A couple of hours passed and eventually we were sent on a short break. The birthday boy would be there soon. We would let him enjoy his day. We're not heartless. Andy had to say goodbye to the DJ as the room emptied and I caught sight of him heading to the restrooms. I followed the pack for a lukewarm coffee and a limp sandwich. As we left the marquee to go out back, a few bodies were clustered around the pool table cake. Amongst them was a tall young man with wavy blond hair and a goofy smile. It was him but I didn't want him to see me yet. I kept out of sight. And I did so want him to see me.

Whilst these rich entitled assholes enjoyed their after-dinner coffee, I looked over at the Birthday Boy. We'd had speeches about going off into the adult world and some amusing stories of his childhood. It was like they were marrying him to adulthood in this flowery temple. He crumpled at the stories, laughing along, old before his time, which of course was why Andy and I were there. He still wore braces on green teeth. When I turned eighteen, it was tequila and boys, and scared stiff we wouldn't get back across the border the next morning. DJ to the Stars played some mellow tunes and nodded his gold-framed dark glasses.

One of the waitresses grabbed another pot of coffee. Helen her name was and she had told me she was dying for a smoke. I winked and took the pot off her. She smiled gratefully and snuck out the back while I made straight for the head table. Birthday Boy was leaning in towards a sweet young thing. I was this young once, but nowhere near as sweet. In a bouncy taffeta dress, she looked pretty. I poured a couple of coffees until I got right behind the pair of them. Both were unaware I was there. I leaned over and whispered in both their ears. "I doubt you'll get laid tonight."

She barely heard me and her face screwed up into a 'what did you say?' expression. Birthday Boy twisted round in his chair, ready to give me a piece of his mind, but it was then that he saw me. I could have been any waitress; black skirt over black stockings, sensible shoes and nice white blouse, hair done up, a little bedraggled from working this gig. But I'm not just anybody, and in that moment he knew it and his face froze. His cheeks had pulled his mouth open to put me in my place but no words came out. Shock will do that to the guys we hunt.

I smiled, coffee pot at the ready. "Hey Tomas. Had a nice life?"

"Thomas?" The girl mispronounced his name slightly, confused at what she just heard. Of course, she knew him as Daryl.

The boy's father sat a few chairs down. He looked at us, his brow furrowed. It was time for me to leave Tomas to it before I drew attention to myself. "Enjoy the party," I said, even meaning it.

Tomas, or Daryl as he was known, leaned forward in his chair. I kept an eye on him as I ducked back to the catering area. He looked around, his shoulders miserably hunched over. The sweet young thing was confused but she placed a gentle hand on his arm. Tomas looked around. The father had turned his attention to an older couple who had appeared at his side. Tomas pulled a linen napkin off his knee and slipped out of his chair, leaving his girlfriend behind. His eyes were on the floor as he skulked away. The girlfriend watched him go, saying nothing.

I saw all this through a gap in the curtain which separated us servers from the guests. A feet away my boss clicked his fingers at me, impatient. I snorted and told him where to go. Then I went after Tomas.

Andy was already on him. Tomas, in his rented tux and shiny shoes, was running for it. I hadn't hung around inside and after blowing my cover as a waitress all I saw was the back of Andy running into a side alley. I stayed on the street. Having lost the apron, I made for the sidewalk and hit it. I barely breathed as I ran by an old warehouse, now fancy apartments. This whole area had been reclaimed by the new gentry and I just ran right through their new neighbourhood in pursuit of one of their sons. Weaving in and out the few people around that afternoon, I cornered the block only to see Tomas barrel out the alleyway with Andy in pursuit.

Tomas yelled out randomly, "Help! Help me!"

I saw a middle-aged woman with a poodle on a leash lift her phone up to dial as she watched the seemingly young man pursued by someone older. As I reached her, I tapped her shoulder to distract her intention. "Police pursuit, ma'am," I said to her in a stern voice. She dropped the phone to her side and she smiled briefly at me. I took this all in an instant, never breaking stride. I must have looked like a cop, like Andy always says I do.

Up ahead, Tomas ran into another building. A rookie mistake, even from him. Andy rammed his broader body through the narrow doorway and a moment later I was inside too. The place was an empty building site. Pocked sheets of plastic drifted where walls should be and I ran across smooth concrete floors to the back of the building. On his back, Tomas writhed on the floor, his tux jacket all dusty. He must have been decked by Andy or even tripped in his stupid new shoes. He was breathing hard and I saw him for what he was now; a pasty kid who never picked up a paper route let alone a football. He was breathing heavily, terrified. His hands were in the air as Andy quietly menaced him; not even out of breath.

As I came up on the two of them, I made a point of not looking behind me. I looked down at Tomas. "You should be afraid you little shit. Why did you run?"

"Are you fucking kidding me?" he roared. The gawky teenager was momentarily gone to be replaced by the Tomas we knew and remembered.

I looked at Andy. He just sort of shrugged with his mouth before asking, "Are you kidding him?"

Staring Andy down like I really meant it. "I'm deadly serious."

He knew what I meant. Andy reached inside his coat and pulled out the Bolt; a small graphite arrow, no bigger than a pencil, with a deadly bronze tip. I took it off him and crouched down beside Tomas, who was still squirming on the floor. His eyes were all red and puffy and I could see the mark on his jaw where Andy must have hit him. I held up the Bolt and Tomas flinched. "Yeah, you know what this is," I told him. He had seen one twice before and now he was getting it again.

Tomas became still. He looked me right in the eye, cool and relaxed. "I'll see you again."

Andy snorted. He already had the pistol crossbow wound up. I took it off him and placed the bolt in its workings. Andy hunkered down to grip Tomas by the shoulders. Tomas just looked at me and sneered, "I've seen you twice already."

Andy chortled. "Don't you know there's a new rule in town?"

Tomas tried to screw his head around to look at Andy, wondering what he meant. By way of explanation, Andy said. "Three strikes, buddy."

I held the crossbow under Tomas' neck; its pistol grip moulded for my hand. He froze but his eyes met mine. I whispered, "Straight to hell." I pulled the trigger and Tomas went limp.

It was late at night as I climbed the fire escape. Darkness brought on cooler air and I followed it inside through an open window. A two-room apartment, this room I'd just stepped into was a crèche. Pink linen, suspended from the ceiling, spread out in an inverted 'V' over an empty crib. Freshly laundered bedding reminded me of my own childhood in a room not unlike this one. Well, this childhood. Previous ones had been a little different. I padded to the open doorway. Staying concealed from the hallway beyond, I tucked in behind the door and looked through the crack.

A TV gibbered away in another room, some cat up a tree crap. And a shadow moved about, a man, and a baby cooed and giggled. I heard splashing; bath-time. Behind the door, a comfortable chair had been pushed into the corner. I quickly moved a stack of diapers and placed them carefully on the floor without making a sound. I sat down and waited.

After a while, the TV was switched off and there was some more moving about. Eventually, all bundled up and sleeping, the baby I had heard came into the room, carried by the man we were after; Martin. With his whole attention on the child, he bounced her gently in his arms before laying her lovingly in the crib. His sleeves were rolled up from having bathed her. Martin leaned in and petted her head. He never looked over his shoulder to the corner once. I sat there waiting. Martin's doorbell rang. He moved his head slightly, but kept his attention on the kid.

When he ignored the bell a second time, I said, "You better get that Martin."

He froze. The doorbell rang a third time and he finally turned round, though slowly, keeping a protective hand on the side of the crib. He caught sight of the open window and I could see his lips move, cursing himself. I recognised the shape of the German words. He was afraid when he finally saw me and made no move when my partner Andy let himself in the front door.

"You make me pick this lock, Martin?" Andy huffed as he found us, his voice loud, pissed off.

"You'll wake the baby," I said and stood up and crossed to the open window. A small breeze hit my back as I leaned on the sill.

"Shit, a baby?" Andy directed this to Martin.

"She's my wife." Martin said it as if we should know.

Andy and I looked at each other. "Sick f-," Andy said. He let the letter just hang in the air like he was going to say the whole word but was stopping himself.

"It's Magda?" My question was to Andy, who shrugged, and then I looked at Martin without concealing my open-mouthed amazement.

"She made it," Martin said. He sounded proud. He stood there, barely fitting his grey pants and cardigan, his hair thinning and white above the ears. And he sounded proud, like he was telling us this to make us like him, like we would be pleased for him. As if it was some kind of achievement to cheat death, miss a few steps, and get ahead of the line.

The moment stretched out for a while until Andy laughed. "This shit is fucked up, Martin. Are you out of your mind?"

"You can't bring her here," I added. I could not believe what he had done, what he and Magda had risked. Leaving aside how plain odd this was, how inappropriate, that his wife was now a baby, it was impossible to comprehend how Martin ever thought he was going to make it work.

He sort of smiled at me. One side of his mouth curled and an eyebrow was raised slightly. "I was a child when I arrived in this time."

"Did you read my mind, Martin?" I asked him. He shrugged slightly, to indicate he had, and that his answer somehow proved it. He kept his position, a hand resting on the crib. He was calculating, though. It was in his eyes as he looked from the door, covered by Andy, and the window covered by me. I tried to see if there was another hidden exit. They always run.

Andy was next to speak. He took a big breath in before saying, "We saw Tomas today, posing as a dude called Daryl."

Martin swallowed. The Adam's Apple on his scrawny neck bobbed. He wanted to know the outcome of our encounter with Tomas but he dared not ask. Maybe he thought we hadn't Bolted him, or he thought we were bluffing, that we were waiting to see if he knew where Tomas was. When Martin looked to me, I gave a tiny shake of my head. *Tomas didn't make it.*

There was a moment before Martin knew what I meant but then he put it together and he just sort of crumbled. It started behind his eyes and spread down to his hips which just gave way. In two steps, Andy was there, caught Martin and just moved his over to the chair. Martin flopped down on its low frame and his eyes greyed out. We had him. We never didn't have him, but he was beaten now. He let out a big sigh and we crowded round him, blocking any attempt to run.

Martin looked me right in the eye, lucid again. "I just wanted to be a step nearer."

I nodded. I understood. I really did, and still do. Me and Andy are further away than ever but it's the price you pay for the life that's chosen you. Martin, and creeps like Tomas, not to mention baby Magda in the crib, wanted something else. Who can blame them?

Andy took the pistol crossbow from under his jacket and primed it. "There are twelve steps, Martin. You wanna get to heaven you gotta get in line."

Martin nodded and watched Andy pull the mechanism back. When he handed it to me, I already had the Bolt in my hand and Martin started breathing a bit harder. Andy reached down to hold him still but Martin flinched and lifted a hand. He stilled his breathing and Andy straightened up without having grabbed the guy. Martin pulled the cuffs of his shirt down. He looked at me. "Will I see you again?"

A tiny shake of my head. *Three strikes and straight to hell.*

Martin swallowed again, his temples pulsed. "And Magda?" He barely managed to say the words, just barely managed to look at his baby wife in the crib.

I huffed a small laugh at such an idiotic question. "We don't Bolt minors, Martin." I put the Bolt in the pistol and put the pistol to his neck. He closed his eyes when I pulled the trigger and his body only flinched slightly as he died.

We stood for a moment in the quiet room. The baby shifted in her crib and cooed lightly. Andy held his hands and cocked his head. "What about the kid?"

This one was on me. "We'll phone the cops and report this murder."

I handed the pistol to Andy. He put it away and shrugged his jacket into a comfortable position. He looked at Martin's lifeless body. "Goddamn Cutters."

SUITCASE OF DREAMS

"ARE YOU JUST off the boat, sir?"

He looks at me and frowns momentarily. Brown eyes flicker in search of the memory to answer my question. He looks back down the pier to see the ferry slip away. It slides easily away from the pier and across the water. We stand on solid ground, away from the wooden pier. A breeze from the sea, a narrow marine lake, cools the air as we meet in warm summer sunshine. He looks tired, as if recently wakened, which if true is a good thing. Sleeping makes the crossing easier.

He puffs out his cheeks and blows out a sigh, my question forgotten. Though I know the answer, I saw him disembark after all, it was asked of him to begin a conversation. His clothes are smart; dressed well in shirt and tie, though no jacket in this fine weather. He rubs his chin, square jawed. There is a hint of stubble. He looks at me and I know what he is thinking. He's wondering why I'm talking to him.

"Would you like a hand with your bags?" I ask.

His hands reach down for his bags, but I can already see

he has none. Puzzled, he looks behind him. The short pier is free of any clutter, let alone anything belonging to him. The main sounds are water splashes, and gulps under the pier, from the wake of the ferry as it continues its journey to the other side. He turns back to me. "I don't seem to..."

"It's quite alright, sir," I say, lifting a hand slightly to gently reassure him. "I can help you. Many visitors arrive without luggage, and I have many varieties."

He smiles uneasily, though gratefully. He has straight white teeth, and must say I find him rather handsome, his bearing agreeable. My time with him will be enjoyable, I think to myself, though professional courtesy forbids me to treat him differently from any other customer. I gesture for him to step away from the pier edge and go further into the town.

We walk together, him looking at the pretty little seaside town which greets his eyes. A terrace of different shaped homes face the sea, each painted in a different vivid colour. His attention is shared between a dark blue three-storey building and its neighbour; smaller and yellow. I ask, "You seem pleased to see this place. Is it similar to one you have visited before?"

He stops and I wait next to him. "Not exactly the same. But yes, I am pleased to be here."

"This way, sir." I hold out an arm to move him further along. "We must reach my shop if I am to sell you some bags."

"Thank you," he says, stepping forward on my lead and giving me a warmer smile this time. Continuing our journey, we turn the corner at the end of the terrace to find the High Street. The road is empty save for us, and shop fronts hold little interest for him. One window, displaying rows of colourful sweetie jars, barely gets a glance from him. He seems more interested in adjusting his tie. "I'm not really here to shop."

"Of course not, sir," I say, "But I'm sure you'll like my

luggage store."

We reach my shop front and I push the door open. A bell above the doorway rings as I beckon him inside and it rings again when he has entered and the door is closed. It is cool inside the shop. Away from the sunshine outside he looks around at the displays. He sees holdalls and handbags but I steer him towards the luggage section. "I'm not really in the mood for shopping," he tells me.

I agree with him. "You've come here to get away from all that."

"I've left it all behind," he says, quite sure of himself in that instant, but the feeling fades and he goes in on himself again, questioning why he should say such a thing. I can see it in his eyes. I'm familiar with this reaction. It's common after all.

I decide to prompt him. "But one must have luggage."

Rubbing the stubble on his chin, he comes to a decision, though he expresses it half-heartedly. "I suppose."

Allowing him, a customer, the space he needs to decide what he wants, I step back. He reviews the stand where I keep the big pieces. He touches a few, but it's clear that nothing is catching his attention. He's not yet ready to make the decision, I suppose. From out of the blue, he says to me, "I've got regrets, you know, about the things I've done."

I pause. "Really?"

He looks at his tie again. It's a sort of mustard colour. He smoothes it against his white shirt and adjusts his collar. In the quietness of the shop, I can hear the bristles of his chin stubble prickle against the material. "I seem to have lived a rather ordinary life." He pauses and looks at me. Confusion flutters across his face. "I don't know why I'm telling you this."

I give him my best smile and don't move from my position, discreetly away from him, my customer. "There's no time for regrets when one is travelling."

"I guess not." His smile, when it comes, is sad, but I recognise relief there too. I've seen it before in other patrons of this shop. I think he's ready now. When I look at the luggage rack, it prompts him to turn his attention back towards it. He quickly finds a piece and slides it out from the rack. We cross to a counter where we examine it. It's convenient to have a large flat space to view the items in the shop. The customer can move around and look at the piece without having to hold it up.

"Good choice." I snip the labels off their plastic ties and discard them in the bin. "Big enough for a long trip, light enough to carry. Are you satisfied with the colour?"

"It's kind of navy, isn't it? I like it." He knocks knuckles on the suitcase's rippled surface. "I like the solid type."

"So do I sir."

His mood brightens and he starts to engage with the process. "Is it a popular model?"

I examine it as I speak. "No, I believe you're the first person to choose this type."

"How much is it?"

I shake my head, and use as soothing a voice as I can. "Nothing. You've already paid."

Satisfied, he smiles broadly at me, showing his straight white teeth. He runs his hands over the item before smoothing down his tie. Sensing his hesitation, I decide to get things moving again. I slide the case off the counter and hold an open palm towards the door. "Shall we go?"

Holding his breath, he nevertheless agrees with a nod. I hold the door open for him. I doubt he hears the bell and we're outside again. It has cooled since we were indoors and the sun is fading behind high cloud blown in from the sea. He follows me up the street. He is blinking and looking around, but he can't seem to focus, his breathing is becoming ragged.

"Not long now, sir. We just need to find a spot." I carry the luggage off the ground, despite it having wheels. We are leaving the empty town behind and arrive at an open piece of flat ground. I stop. He looks around, seeing nothing.

"Is this it?" He's not surprised, just asking me the question.

"All our choices bring us here," I tell him, placing the luggage gently on the ground. I kneel down beside it, laying it flat, and pressing the buttons which release the catch.

His breath catches and I see him look around. Mist has blown in. Sea breeze reaches up to us. From experience, I know that his view of the town is obscured by this mist and he is beginning to feel disconnected from his surroundings; panicking almost. Smoothly, I stand and place a hand on his shoulder. "Keep your attention on the suitcase."

His brown eyes still when I speak before moving to the case. It lies open, showing its clean dark interior. He says to me, "There's not much room."

"There's all the space you'll need," I tell him as simply as I can.

The mist moves again in the breeze and I hope he doesn't glimpse the row upon row of suitcases lying flat and closed. Sometimes they do and I must handle their reaction. He looks at me. His breathing has stilled. "Will I dream?"

I don't know the answer to this question, though I am often asked. I swallow and nod. My hand is still on his shoulder. "Yes, you will dream."

I let him go. He rubs his chin stubble again and breathes out. He steps into the suitcase and lies down. He pulls the lid down himself, something not all customers do. Of course, I secure the latches myself, crouching down again. I wait for a moment in that position and think of him. As predicted, our time together was pleasant.

I tap the surface of the suitcase gently, before standing. My knees barely make it but I'm soon upright. I pat myself down. I've become a little dusty and need to make sure that I am presentable. It would not do for someone to visit my shop and find otherwise.

The mist has gone and the sun is poking through the high cloud, ready to shine again. Beyond the town, from my elevated position amongst the rows of suitcases, I see the pier reach into the water. The ferry is returning. I head off towards it, ready to meet my next customer of the day.

GOOD MORNING, NEIGHBOUR

I KISS MY wife goodbye. She straightens my tie before smiling and waving at me as I walk down our path. Our son stands to her left, still in his pyjamas. He rubs his eyes sleepily and clutches a teddy. I smile broadly at them. I am next to my car. It is a blue station wagon. Opening the car door, I wave again then my briefcase is on the seat next to me. The car has started up and I am driving out of my driveway.

On leaving our street, I turn left onto Main Street. People are going about their morning business. A yellow car passes, travelling in the opposite direction. Checking the traffic behind me, I catch sight of myself in the mirror and I adjust my glasses. Sunlight pours through the window and warms my arms. I wave as I recognise a neighbour pushing a stroller down the sidewalk; her child shakes a rattle in the air. Another neighbour parks his green car outside the drugstore and ambles inside.

The only light on Main Street is suspended over the intersection. It is at red. Slowing my blue station wagon to a halt, I wait behind a black SUV; its darkened windows concealing the occupants. A high-pitched squeal behind me, then to the left of me, and now in front of me, as a red sports car appears from nowhere, rounds me, and then smacks into the black SUV in front. The driver of the red car jumps out of his door and is firing a pistol, side-on with the handle pointing off to the right.

I am alarmed and don't know what to do. My jaw lies open and my eyes must be popping out of my head. Gunfire explodes around me. The driver of the black SUV gets out. He is enormous, barely fitting into his black suit. He is firing a machine gun. Despite his size, the gun is still huge and its bullets punch great holes into the red car. Neither man has yet been hit by a bullet. My windshield is holed twice, two round circles that spread out in a jagged pattern. The bullets have not hit me.

Police sirens pulse up ahead and blue and red lights flicker into my eyes. The two men stop firing at each other and turn to face the direction of the police. Two black and white cars land on the intersection and the officers are on their feet, leaning into the gap between their car door and the vehicle itself, firing their weapons. Machine gun and angled-pistol fire is hammered back at them. The man from the red car is jumping up and down, firing casually. The man with the machine gun is poised, anchoring his feet and firing with more care. Neither takes cover.

My windshield takes some more hits and I duck. Glass shatters all around me, crunching onto the seats and floor. Cowering beneath the steering wheel, I flip the car into reverse and lift my foot from the brake, feeling the car begin to move backwards. The gun battle continues. Warily, I lift my head to see through the space where the window had been. A police officer is falling to the ground. In that instant, through the gaping hole where my windshield should be, I see his face contort in pain, as he clutches his chest and crumples backwards. His body goes slack. I press the accelerator.

My car swerves erratically backwards until I see my neighbour, leaving his green car to go into the drugstore. I shout out, "Get in your car! Run!" But he does not hear me. I see my other neighbour with her stroller. The child rattles its toy and gurgles at the sky. I shout out to her, "Get in! Get in!" She ignores me and continues along the sidewalk. I realise she is going towards the intersection. I press my horn but she continues, oblivious. I kick the brake to halt the car.

I look through my windshield up ahead; my windshield, it is intact. Rapping it with a knuckle shows it to be whole. I look to the seat beside me and see only my briefcase. There is no shattered glass there, or on my lap, or on the floor. Looking up ahead again, I see the intersection. I can hear myself breathing. The intersection is clear. The light is green and traffic flows through. There is no gun battle. I wait for a moment, breathing and listening to the engine idling. A black SUV overtakes me and cruises down Main Street.

I put the car in drive and follow the black SUV. A yellow car passes, travelling in the opposite direction. The neighbour with the stroller continues with her journey. The child rattles the toy. My other neighbour locks his green car and goes into the drugstore. I see now that he is locking it before turning to the building. I notice this for the first time and that the child in the stroller is a girl. I hadn't seen this earlier. I arrive at the intersection behind the SUV. A familiar high-pitched squeal and the red sports car rounds me to collide with the SUV. The occupant gets out, but this time it's a woman who gets out and not a man firing a pistol side-on. She is a tall blonde in a red dress, a long split up each thigh, with silver pistols in holsters where her garters should be. She takes all the time in the world to ready herself. She even looks at me for a moment and winks. Then the shooting begins. A pistol in each hand she is coolly firing at the SUV. The driver of the black SUV is the same burly male as before. He is firing a machine gun.

This time I do not hesitate. At full speed, I reverse up Main Street. I see my neighbour at his green car outside the drugstore and I scream at him to run but he ignores me again. Our other neighbour and her little girl in the stroller head back down Main Street. I lean on the horn and know that my shouting is useless but what else can I do? The yellow car passes me on the other side and this encourages me to change direction. I pull on the wheel and my blue station wagon lurches round in a circle. The tyres squeal as the vehicle is flung round and amazingly I don't lose any speed and I start to move forward away from the intersection.

I speed into my driveway and run up to the front door. I am panicking. My wife is at the door. She smiles at me and adjusts my tie. Our son stands at her knees. He is clutching a teddy bear and rubbing his eyes. I don't understand how they have just stood there since I left them. I try to talk to my wife as she smiles and adjusts my tie. "We have to call the police. Something very strange is happening." She smiles and reaches out for my tie, but I grasp her hands in mine. "What are you doing?"

I realise I am shouting. Our son rubs his eyes and begins to yawn. I look at my wife. She is still smiling. I want to grab her and handle her inside but she seems so fragile. She is wearing a flower pattern apron over a yellow jersey and a puffed skirt. Her eyes, though shining with love for me, are flat, like they are painted on. She looks through me almost. Blonde hair is flicked away from her face as she smiles at me. Her hands have been removed from my grip and she adjusts my tie. I see, as if noticing for the first time, that her nose crinkles as she takes enjoyment from this morning ritual.

Our son rubs his eyes and begins to yawn. His eyes widen. Something behind me has taken his attention. My wife sees it too. She screams. Her hands are on my shoulders and she kicks one of her feet in the air behind her. I turn around and see a gas tanker, a huge truck, crash through our neighbour's house; straight through. It tears up his yard and is coming towards our yard, towards us. The cab lurches to the side and the tanker begins to jack-knife. The truck's tyres chug in ever increasing volume as the driver tries to right the vehicle. I see his expression beneath a red cap as he panics. Finally, the truck is over on its side and it explodes.

The sound is enormous and the blast knocks us all off our feet. Heat washes over us and a yellow fireball pushes into the air mutating into a black cloud in the shape of a mushroom. Gunfire crackles through the sound as the red sports car from earlier spins into our street pursued by the black SUV. The man in the red sports car, the first driver I saw earlier, is behind the wheel. The driver of the SUV is leaning out his window and firing his machine gun. Police sirens from Main Street can be heard.

I look at my wife. She is alarmed and clearly doesn't know what to do. Our son is crying, standing again, his teddy still in his hand, though held loosely at his side. My wife's eyes search mine for an answer. I tell her, "We have to go." She nods, absent-mindedly, and I help her to her feet. I lift our son up and hold him close. Keeping low, we run towards the back of the house. Leaving in the car is not an option because of the tanker and the gun battle which both block our way out. Flocks of police cars move in, their white doors open for the officers to spill out and fire at the combatants.

I hold our son in my arm and hold my wife's hand as we enter our back yard. Water spits out a sprinkler as we cross the lush grass. We reach the fence and run along to the gate. My wife unlatches it with her free hand and we are out into the alley, leaving the sound of gunfire behind. I look up and already the cloud has dispersed into the air, leaving only a blue sky. Looking back to the alley, a dog sniffs around a lamp-post then scampers off.

A man walks up the alley towards us. His shirt is rolled up at the sleeves and he carries a newspaper. He is smiling. My wife is in a state of total panic. She clutches my hand. Our son, still in pyjamas, buries his head in my shoulder. As the man approaches, I say to him, "Turn around! Go back!"

As if he did not hear me, the man smiles at me and says, "Good morning, neighbour."

I go to stop him, to say something more, but my wife pulls at my hand, saying, "We have to go. Go now!"

I agree. At the end of the alley, the street is quiet at first but as we pause, considering which way to go, the red sports car rushes past. For a moment, I feel like everything slows down and I see the driver behind the wheel. It is the blonde in the red dress. She smiles and winks at me before gunning her car on. Gunshots bring the moment back to normal speed and the black SUV hurtles past, its driver leaning out of the window and firing his machine gun. I see for the first time that he is balding at the crown of his head and the rest of his hair is close cropped. His black suit is old and frayed at the lapels. His tie hangs loose around the open collar of a grubby white shirt. All this I see in a heartbeat as bullets zing and smack around us. I don't know how we are not hit.

When the cars have gone, we cower at the corner of the alley as police cars rush after the two vehicles. I look at my wife. She is scared but is beginning to come to her senses. She checks on our boy. He is unhurt. My wife tells me this with a nod of her head and a relieved sigh. The man with rolled up sleeves is still in the alley and he wishes us a good morning as he heads off with his newspaper. My wife and I exchange a look which means we don't understand what is happening but we no longer care about that. All we care about is our son.

I ask her, "Where shall we go?"

"The bridge." She is sure about this, so we go.

We walk through many streets, some I know, but most I don't. Everywhere we go black SUVs and red sports cars are involved in a deadly chase. A few people are like us, frightened and scared, and running away from the mayhem and confusion. But others, most we see in fact, are like the man with the rolled-up sleeves and newspaper. In fact, they are like my wife and son were when I went back home. They are impassive, unconcerned, sometimes cheerful at best. We see men who can only be brothers of the man with the newspaper. They are dressed differently, some with rolled down sleeves, or even a tie and hat, but unmistakeably relatives of the man in the alley. We don't know what to make of this so we keep going.

"Which bridge are we going to?" I ask when I realise my wife is leading us in a direction I'm unsure of.

"It's this way," she says. Her voice is a forced whisper. Her knees are bent as she makes quick progress despite her white high heeled shoes. Our son's head remains buried in my shoulder. His teddy is missing, dropped somewhere behind us. She pulls at my hand as we make our way through a less affluent area. Burnt-out cars litter the street. Wooden houses sit back from scrubby lawns. An old woman sits on her rocking chair and smiles at us. She seems flat to me, unrounded, but she smiles and waves at us from her raised porch. Flaked paintwork speckles the front of her home. Tiles are missing from her roof. My son lifts his head and waves back at her silently. This makes her very happy. As we leave her, she has stopped rocking and holds her palms together in front of her mouth like she is thinking about something.

The sun pushes through hazy smog. It is hot and I am becoming tired from carrying my son. Behind us, the sound of car chases is diminishing. Up ahead, two youths confront another boy, pushing him against a wall. My wife pulls us up a different street to avoid them. My glasses slip down my nose. Our son strokes my shirt where the sleeve meets my arm above the elbow.

Buildings begin to thin out. We're in more of an industrial area now. Blocky buildings have been shuttled in amongst one another, threaded by alleys. Thin streams of water trickle down slopes. A black SUV is parked outside a building advertised as "Inner City Ink Inc". The script is lurid and stylised. A bald-headed man stands outside the door smoking a cigarette. His left foot is placed on the wall behind him while his right is planted on the ground. Revealed by a white T-shirt, tattoos cover his arms. He ignores us.

"We're nearly there." My wife looks both ways before dragging us across the road. There is no traffic. Up ahead, the smog is much thicker. An old man with a walking frame walks on the other side of the road, but is going in the same direction as us. He is making slow progress and we leave him quickly behind. I begin to worry that we are wasting our time. We have seen many police cars and did not attempt to slow one down or stop it. We should have done that.

There are no buildings now. The sidewalk we are on borders a very wide road, with multiple lanes. No traffic in either direction disturbs the surface. Ahead, the smog has become much thicker but I can see support columns with cables running down in parallel lines to reach a road. "Is this the bridge?" I ask.

My wife nods urgently and grips my hand tighter. We slow our pace and walk towards the structure. Our son lifts his head and indicates he wants down by making his body rigid. I let him slide to the ground and his slippers touch the sidewalk. I move him between my wife and me. We hold a hand each. As we near the bridge, I can make out the support columns rise into the smog in a giant 'H' shape. Thick cables support the road but below that, where I would expect to see what the bridge is crossing, like a river or the sea, there is only more smog. Swirling around, it is all around us now. We cannot see the other side of the bridge. All sound is muffled but there are people here.

An older man, thin and dressed in slacks and a polo shirt leans against a chain link fence. He looks at us with a puzzled expression. A young couple rush up behind us, clutching hands, and run panicked onto the bridge and into the smog. Very quickly, they disappear from view. I am unsure about us going any further. I stop and ask my wife, "Why this way?"

Her eyes twitch about. Her free hand goes up to her mouth and she taps fingers on her chin, thinking about the answer. "It seemed the right thing to do." She looks up and sees the old man with the walking frame. He is nearly on the bridge now and begins to fade in amongst the grey fog as he steps carefully forward, lifting the frame, placing it in front of him, taking a step, and lifting the frame again. "See, he's going that way," says my wife. "We should go this way."

I'm still not sure. Our son is becoming anxious. We are at the threshold of the bridge. I look behind us and see more people coming towards us. Some are shuffling, where others are more determined. None take any notice of us. The older man in slacks and polo shirt is the only one interested in us. He shakes his head slowly at me. I turn to look back at the bridge. I hold my hand out and it seems to be swallowed by the fog, obscured from view. My wife looks puzzled. My hand feels cold and I pull it back. It returns to view but it seems flatter somehow, like the shadows have been rubbed out. There's very little light because of the smog but my wife and our son seem rounded while my hand looks bland. I put it in my pocket, take a deep breath, and feel sensation returning to my hand. I pull it back out and look at it again. It seems fine, normal, like before. Our son releases himself from our hands and goes to step forward.

"I wouldn't let him do that." The older man in slacks

and polo shirt has stepped forward. I place hands on the boy's shoulders and steer him back to his mother.

"Why should I not let him do that?" I ask the man. He has come right up to us. I see that his face is deeply lined and weathered. He is wearing a white golfing cap, square on his head. I had not noticed that before. In reply to my question, he makes a backward nod to indicate we should look at the bridge, which we do.

The young couple who had made to flee over the bridge were now returning, though they are walking slower. Their hands are still together but there is less urgency. They hold hands in a more relaxed manner and they are no longer running, but walking more normally. Returning from the bridge and not running away to cross it, their expressions are glassy, removed from their thinking and they seem flat, their movements mechanical almost. As they pass us they smile and the young man says, "Good morning, neighbour."

Without us returning the greeting, the couple move on, back towards the city. I turn to the older man in the cap and say to him, "What just happened?"

He looks at me for a moment, with that same quizzical look. He says, "How did it happen for you? Did you do something different?" His tone is casual as if I should understand what he is talking about. My expression must give away that I have no idea what he means. He scratches his chin. "What did you do today?"

I look to my wife. She is as stunned as I am. I tell the man about driving out our street, the intersection, the gun battle, the windshield breaking and reforming, going back to the intersection and seeing the same scene but with different people, then returning home. With a hand, he stops me speaking, "You went home? To your family?"

"My wife and our son," I tell him. I have our son by the shoulders, held in front of me. My wife stands closer to me. "Why are you asking me this?"

Instead of answering my question, the man asks me, "What did you do yesterday?"

I start to answer but no words come out. I look to my wife. She puts her mouth into a downturned smile and shakes her head. She cannot remember either. I say to the man, "Who are you?"

"I'm just a guy that's been looking at this bridge for a while," he says and moves to get a better view. From through the fog, a figure is starting to emerge and we hear a metallic click followed by a few shuffles. As we listen, the man in the polo shirt tells us about his morning, how he was in his yard, mowing his lawn, when all of a sudden a truck smashed through his house and jack-knifed on his lawn. A black SUV and a red sports car crashed through his fence and the occupants were shooting at each other. He could see his wife in the kitchen get blown back as bullets blasted the window. Somehow he managed to avoid the bullets and make his way inside. He found his wife on the floor in a pool of blood. Already the sound of shots was fading. His wife's eyes looked into the distance and she didn't seem concerned in anyway, perhaps even peaceful, but just before she died, she looked at him. Alarm appeared across her face and she cried out to him before she rattled and passed away.

He had held her hand for a while. When he stood up, he looked outside, through an unbroken pane of glass to find his yard was whole. There was no damage, no truck, no SUV or sports car. Everything in his yard was just as it was earlier. He ran outside because he could not believe what he was seeing. His mower lay gently idling on the lawn. When he reached it, it moved slightly and some tufts of grass flew out behind it. Movement in the corner of his eye, from the direction of his kitchen, forced him back inside only to find something even stranger.

"What was it, sir?" my wife asks. She is enthralled by the man's story.

"It was my wife," says the man, "up and about as if nothing had happened. She wasn't hurt or injured, and her eyes were flat and colorless. She looked at me and smiled."

"What did you do next?" I shuffle on my feet.

"I came here," says the man, laughing, and flipping his hands out to indicate the bridge. "Some uncontrollable panic led me here."

"To the bridge," my wife says, wistful, like she was remembering her reason for making us come here.

"That's right, the bridge," says the man. "See, I did something different today, and other folks are the same. Look at this guy." He indicates out at the bridge, towards the clicking and shuffling sound. It is the old man with the walking frame who had crossed earlier. He is returning, even slower than before, emerging from the smog but still distant. He lifts the frame, places it in front, then takes two shuffles to catch up, and then lifts the frame again. The man in the cap says, "He's done something different today, and for some reason, he couldn't help himself but come here."

We watch the old man come closer. The colours of his clothes appear out the smog, but pale and flat, like a bad drawing. I swallow. "What does this all mean?"

"I can't tell you that," says the man, "but think back to the people you saw at the intersection. It was like they weren't taking it seriously. Am I right?"

"Like a game?"

"All I can tell you is what I see," says the man. "It was like it didn't mean nothin' to them and we don't mean nothin' to them. Half the people I seen today look the same, just staring into space. Then something happens and they come here."

"That's right, that's right," says my wife. Her demeanour is anxious, like she is on the verge of grasping the point. "We come here to be refreshed. To come back new and ready."

"What are you talking about?" I'm yelling at her and grab her arms as she flails about. Our son moves away, scared, and the old man in the cap keeps a hold of him in case he runs off onto the bridge. I am still yelling. "How did you know to bring us here?"

"We've got no choice!" my wife shouts. She is crying. Tears stream down her face. "We can go back there with all our memories and try and survive or we go out there and be refreshed."

I relax. Back there, in town, at our home, we would have cars crashing into our yard and people shooting police officers, but here we would forget. All we would have to do is cross that bridge. Like the young couple who ran across so frantically but returned so calmly, we could do the same. "Could that be right?" I ask the man in the cap and slacks and polo shirt.

"I think your wife is right," he says to me. We see from the direction of the town, the old lady from the porch rocking chair. She is bent over and can hardly walk, but she is trotting towards the bridge and the smog.

The old man with the walking frame keeps coming closer. He is the figure we have seen and heard approaching, but much nearer now. He lifts the frame, places it in front of him, takes two shuffles to catch up, and then lifts the frame again. He looks towards us, almost through us, as if his eyes are not quite focused. His features are flat and unresponsive but he looks like he could be the brother of the man we have just been talking to, and who is still right next to me, and is wearing a cap, slacks and a polo shirt. The old man with the walking frame smiles.

He says, "Good morning, neighbour."

ZOMBIE PARK

WE WATCH THE video on a large screen. There is no sound and the image flickers in the darkened lecture room. No-one speaks. I want to take in every detail. At first, all we can see is the control panel of the aircraft. Blue gridded panels sit either side of what looks like a map screen. Funnily, I notice the symmetry of it. The camera is attached to the pilot's shoulder and it bobs the image around. We only have a brief sight of the heads-up display and the horizon beyond as it flips from level to angled as the pilot moves the stick and his Typhoon fighter responds. A light begins to flash on a sharp-cornered square button and, a heartbeat later, the pilot has made a decision and ejected. A flurry of soundless energy escapes and the scene blurs as the pilot is wrenched from his position.

There is a weightless pause before the horizon comes into view on this massive screen and it's clear the pilot is now out of the aircraft and in the air. We catch a glimpse of the fighter jet falling away, spinning a coiled exhaust as it falls towards the old shopping centre. There is a jerk and we see the sky but then we see the pilot's body and the ground below. His slow pace of falling means the parachute has deployed. Clad in a green flight suit, his body is lean and we catch sight of his helmeted head as he himself glimpses the ground. He's heading for an open area of grass dotted with a few clumps of trees. The grass must be long because it sways in a breeze and waves of movement pass across the whole area.

I lean in closer, forearms on the bench in front of me, and peer into the screen. Waves of grass seem to part and create a massive pattern forming a 'D' shape before it moves again. There is a small tut behind me. I think the person who made it has realised that what he is seeing on the screen is not grass, but human bodies. As the parachuting pilot nears the swaying mass of people, we see he is trying to make manoeuvres to avoid them. He tugs on the parachute and his target position moves, but the swarm on the ground moves to meet him. We begin to see ravaged faces, ragged clothes, and outstretched arms.

The pilot is panicking on screen. His legs are kicking as if he's trying to run away but he continues to fall. In the room, we're becoming uneasy. We know what's going to happen. He is near the ground now and we can make out hundreds of faces, red greedy eyes, rotting teeth biting the air in anticipation. There is a glimpse of the shopping centre in flames because the abandoned Typhoon has crashed into it. And in the last few moments of the pilot's life, grasping bony fingers reach out for him as he drops helplessly into their midst.

Mercifully, the screen fades and the lights come up. Jerry, our host and trainer, steps forward into the centre of the now-white screen. Unlike the other people who work here, he's not wearing black army-style clothes and a square skip cap. He wears chinos and a green logoed polo shirt. All morning, his smile has been wide and his teeth are bright white, but now his face is serious.

"Welcome," says Jerry. "To Zombie Park."

In the truck, we're all a bit quiet though there's a lot of

engine noise and we sit in two rows facing each other. Canvas panels keep the view hidden. We were told to bring our own boots. I'm wearing comfy hiking shoes I got from the internet. The rest of our outfits are mock-ups of military uniforms. Only a huge American calling himself Gus is fully done up in his own gear. He wears a wide brimmed army hat which is pinned up on one side. He chews something behind massive jaws and he smiles under a broad moustache. To hide my nervousness I look away but this only encourages him to talk to me. He leans over and says through whatever it is he's eating, "Where you from, kid?"

I shrug, intimidated his size and confidence. "Here, Edinburgh."

He raises his chin in understanding. "Scottish then. You been out there? Before it happened?"

"To Livingston? Few times. My cousin lived there." We're heading there in the truck now, leaving Edinburgh on the old A71 road. The towns and villages between here and there have all been evacuated and we're officially in the Cleared Zone. My cousin Dave lived near the shopping centre we saw in the video and we hung about in the games shop while his mum went to the supermarket. I haven't heard from Dave in a number of years. This American thinks it's funny.

Laughing, Gus claps me on the arm. "You'll maybe see him again, kid."

He leans back in his seat, happy with his joke. We're all sitting in a row like we're going to some battle, which of course we are, but the taste of it is disgusting. We've had the training. Of course, this Gus guy could already shoot well. Others in the group even had some experience during the outbreak. Lisa, a woman from the North East, claimed at dinner one night to have 'popped' seventeen of them. Like me, she's a lottery winner. Our numbers came up and we won the trip of a lifetime. Gus has paid for this 'vacation' with his own money. I've kept quiet. I just want to get in there.

I can feel us barrelling through the darkness to this town in Central Scotland, leaving my hometown of Edinburgh. Other places got hit harder, so they say, but there's not much left of Wester Hailes where I grew up. I was in the cinema the first time I saw one of them. He seemed like a normal schemie sort of guy, with the low slung trackie bottoms and the hat at a stupid angle. He was just sort of standing there, looking depressed, then he just attacked this lassie for no reason. I'd seen something similar before outside the library but this was different, more frenzied and he bit right into her neck. I knew what he was straight away, even before someone shouted "Zombie!" and we all got off our marks. And that was the end of the movie.

There's a change in the engine noise and I hear what I think is shouting. Through a gap in the canvas coverings I see we've come inside a massive gated corridor. Outside, there are some people holding up banners and shouting their heads off. They're outside the fence but still in the Cleared Zone. Gus humphs a laugh. "Protesters," he says, half to himself, then shouts out louder, "They can't feel nothin'!"

A couple of our fellow travellers laugh at him but I see Lisa just curls her lip slightly. "Some of those people have family in there, wandering about." She has to shout to be heard.

Gus just shrugs. "You're comin' in too, sweetheart. If anyone has a problem, ya can call my solicitor." He says the last word in what he thinks is a British accent. Lisa sets her jaw to one side, folds her arms, and looks at the canvas ceiling.

Finally, we're out the truck and into the cool autumn air. There's no breeze and apart from our movement there are no other sounds. We've fallen in, army style like we've been trained. Sergeant McIntyre has ordered us to stand easy;

feet apart with hands clasped behind the back. Her face gives us a proud look as she looks us up and down. We've had a week of this and she's telling us we're ready now. One afternoon and it will all be over. I wonder how I'll feel afterwards.

We're inside a small fenced area. Jerry appears from a portakabin next to the wire. Carrying a clipboard, he's in his chinos and green polo shirt with a red ZP stitched into the left breast. The stylized P seems to appear out of a slashed Z. I've been studying marketing at college and interested in such things. You even find yourself saying 'zee' instead of 'zed'. We've heard all his stories of being a Holiday Rep in Ibiza when the outbreak happened. He says he barely made it out alive and now he works here. Next summer, he hopes to go back out there. ZP Inc have a park there too, you know.

"Good morning, everyone," he says breezily. "Not long until you get in there. I just need to run over some of the safety information." He points over at a large board fixed to the wire. In large bold type, under the ZP logo of course, is a big list of rules we've had drummed into us since the beginning. He reads through them. "One: This is a live environment. Two: The Infected are in the Park. Three: You are about to enter the Park. Four: Danger of death is more likely than serious injury. Five: If you are infected, you will stay in the Park and become part of the Attraction. Six: Head shots are the most effective way of stopping one of the Infected. Seven: Do not shoot each other, except in an extreme emergency. Eight: You enter at your own risk. Nine: Have fun."

After being given the chance to leave, which none of us take, and signing a final sheet to that effect, we enter the Park. I'm in a three-man team with Lisa and Gus. We've practiced all week. Sergeant McIntyre was quite blunt about why I'm with these two: I'm the most observant, Gus can really shoot, and Lisa is fully motivated to terminate the Infected. We've each been given MP5s, the sort of thing you used to see the police carrying at airports. It looks like a machine gun but it fires single shots instead of a million. The idea is to take out the Infected, not pepper you and your team. Like we've been trained, we hold it across ourselves, with the muzzle pointed down, our finger poised over the trigger guard. When we leave the final gate, Gus steps ahead while Lisa covers the rear. I'm in the middle, looking all around. We are quiet, our knees slightly bent, and we cover the ground quickly.

Let out in the part of town known as Craigshill, we are moving through an old park. A wide river is to the left of us and high buildings are on our right. Assured this immediate area is kept clear of the Infected, I don't feel assured and I can feel my body tingle. I want to run back and bang on the gate but I keep going in with the others to face the Infected. As we reach the building, we head up a cracked tarmac road to a main road, furry with weeds. Some burnt out cars are dotted at odd angles.

We're inside the town proper now, though still far from where the Typhoon pilot parachuted to his death. Low buildings meet us. They face each other in long strips up the hill. Every leaf moved by a breath of wind startles me. Gus stumbles slightly as his boot finds a pothole and I jangle with fright. He holds up a hand and we stop. I look Lisa in the eye and there is something feral there, wolfish and dark. The corners of her mouth smile at me. We look to Gus. He gestures towards the corner of a partly fallen down house. We nod and follow him over there. Already my calves are hurting from moving quickly in a slightly crouched position.

Finally we are there and rest our shoulders against the wall. Gus is panting. He has hauled his large body up here and is already feeling it. Lisa leans in and hisses. "This is madness. We're already pinning ourselves against a wall."

She's pissed off with Gus for having set himself up as the leader and she's right about our position. We can't see a thing except where we've just came from. Gus nods and sticks an eye round the corner. He looks back at us, nods then steps out. I follow and we're in the open again. The old fallen down bungalow we've just been behind fronts onto a walkway with an identical facing of buildings. These houses form terraces with a paved walkway in between. We form up, me in the middle, with Lisa behind. As I look ahead over Gus's shoulder, I see one in the flesh.

For the first time in over six months, I see one step out from behind a gap in the terrace. He's ragged, clothes all torn, eyes bulging grey and red, cheeks sunken in, skin torn and haggard. It's one of the Infected and it lumbers towards us with a breathy urgency. "I got it!" calls out Gus and he shoots. It takes him three shots before he even hits it in the shoulder and another two before he hits the head and the Infected guy falls down.

Gus rushes up to see his kill. Lisa curses and we go after him. Gus has dropped his stance, and holds his gun across him. I'm sure he would have dropped it if it weren't for the strap. Lisa and I keep our formation, watching out for each other and more Infected. For the first time, I've got the MP5 at my shoulder and I'm staring down the barrel. As Gus dances around the fallen Infected I cover the body in case it moves again, while Lisa scans the area. She's managed to put herself into what's known in a combat situation as the dominant position and I feel cool under her watch. The body on the ground is quiet.

"Hot dog," says Gus. "I got myself one. He's actually finally really dead this time. I got you now motherfucker."

It's like he's taunting the prone body. Suddenly he shouts up into the air and lets off a couple of rounds.

Lisa is mad. "Cut it out! You're making too much noise."

"What the hell are you worried about? Draggin' more of

'em here? That's what we came for!" Gus fires off another shot.

We all pause on that for a moment. Lisa sighs in agreement and all find ourselves smiling at each other. He's right. This is what we came for.

I'm on point as we head towards The Mall, a small neighbourhood shopping centre. We're in a good rhythm now. Gus is at the rear and Lisa is right behind me. I've got my MP5 at my shoulder. Leaning into it, I keep my knees bent as I step forward. We're quite out in the open as we approach the low building. To our left is an office block and what looks like an exploded public toilet. An exhausted old pub has fallen off its stilts onto the courtyard below. We ignore the boarded up supermarket and head for the main entrance to the Mall. A large roller door is half opened. Rubbish has spilled out from the opening and been blown around. I pause to get my bearings. Lisa taps me on the shoulder and then points with a side on palm towards the roller door; *Go*.

I'm shaking with excitement as I start to move again. We reach the roller door. It's up at my chest. Gus and Lisa position themselves with their backs to it, their weapons at their shoulders. Cautiously, I crouch down and peer into the building. Silent inside, there is a hellish smell. It's not just the discarded trash. Lisa lowers her weapon as she turns to me. I nod. With a glint in her eye, she nods back. I step inside and straighten, raising the gun. Lisa comes in straight after me, with Gus following.

Everything is ruined. What isn't broken has been burned. The few small shops have been long looted. Bizarrely fresh and blue, a display stand from an earlier lottery system sits outside the door of an old newsagent. A few tattered magazines are on the floor of an otherwise empty shop. We make our way through, Lisa just behind me, Gus covering the rear. Halfway through, we catch each other's eyes and make an agreement.

Gus is the first to speak. "Ain't nothin' here, guys."

Lisa nods. "Shall we go?"

I relax. We all do, changing our postures and beginning the walk back to the roller door. Just as I'm about to say something, we hear a shuffle behind us. In one movement, we all whirl round, weapons at the ready. I can feel sweat on my body and can even smell myself, clammy and unclean. There is nothing for a moment, but then an Infected woman shuffles out of the old post office. She has no shoes on and her feet are all ragged from having shuffled around here for months. Her grubby outfit is an old skirt and top. Her hair is lank and falling away from an exposed scalp. I'm ready to run.

"You're on, point." Lisa taps me on the shoulder again and steps back.

My breakfast of eggs and bacon starts to lift in my stomach and I just want out of there. The smell has gotten worse since she appeared; a foul rotten stench. Trying to move my feet, I somehow can't shift. I swallow in a dry throat even though I feel like heaving. The infected woman stops and just looks at us. It's like her eyes are focused on us but it's also like there's nothing behind those eyes. Whatever was there before has been replaced by a cold emptiness. I want to help her somehow, but keep staring at her down the barrel. I pull the weapon closer to me, trying to decide what to do. I try to think about my training: head shot lethal, chest shot will slow them down.

"You got this, kid," says Gus, quietly. "Take the shot."

The infected woman cocks her head to the side and her eyes narrow, almost like she's thinking about something. Then she comes at me, fast.

I pull on the trigger and straight away I know I've done it too quick. I've jerked on the trigger instead of squeezing it. A massive crack thunders around this enclosed space and the infected woman is rocked on her heels. Somehow, I've hit her in the chest. But she recovers quickly and comes at me again. A howl comes out of her. I take a couple of steps back and feel Lisa's hand on my back, stopping me. Gus is stepping forward, sighting the infected woman, but I squeeze the trigger and I take the infected woman's head off. There's a spray of grey blood and she falls onto the tiled floor, her howl silenced.

I'm breathing heavily. The MP5 is still at my shoulder. Gus is going forward, passing the infected woman, scanning the other shop units for more Infected. Lisa puts a hand on my left shoulder. I think about the weapon but I've already flipped the safety back on and my finger is off the trigger. All I need to do is relax.

There are no other Infected people in The Mall. We head back to the roller door. Lisa is on point. She ducks down and we follow her. Outside, I'm glad of the fresh air. We stand with our backs to the roller door. The three of us are ready, but our weapons are pointing down. We're facing a downwards slope. In the distance, we can see the Pentland Hills, covered in grass and heather. Nearer to us, we can see the town of Livingston spread out before us. Once, it was a town in Scotland, now it's the playground of ZP Incorporated: Zombie Park.

A scattered group of the Infected are shuffling towards us, awoken by the sound of gunfire and the scent of our fresh blood.

"You ready?" Gus asks.

"I'm ready," I say and we look at Lisa.

She gives us her wolfish smile. "Let's go kill some people."

GIANTS

"GIANTS LIVE UNDER here," said Dad.

I laughed and shook my head. "They do not." Smacking the back of my spade on the vent caused its slats to close and the hissing stopped. It was an easy one.

Dad did the next one. It was bigger for a start, broader and wider. He raised his much larger shovel and smacked it down. The smaller vent next to it hissed and struggled, wisps of steam threaded through the gaps. I raised my spade in readiness but Dad held out his hand. "Wait! That one needs opening."

I groaned, slumping my shoulders. Already at fourteen years of age, I must have been becoming stroppy and difficult to deal with. "How can you even tell?"

Dad came over, his boots scraping the grass. He was grinning at me, his massive frame silhouetted against the grey sky. We were near one of the seven stone pillars dotted across the land which marked where the groups of vents were. He crouched down beside me as I rested hands on both knees, staring down at the vent. He held out a weathered hand and pointed a grimy fingernail at fatigued metal. He spoke gently to me. "It's the steam coming out. It needs to escape. Once it's done, the vent will attempt to close. When air is being drawn back inside, you get a different sound, like breathing in."

He gestured for me to do it. I breathed in, the backward sigh sounding in my chest. I held it in.

"That's when it needs closed," he went on. "Now breathe out."

I needed to anyway and the air in my lungs burst out through my mouth. It felt hot and I had to try and catch my breath afterwards. Dad laughed, "So what do you think is happening? Under here?"

I looked around. As far as we could see, the mound of grass dotted with vents was just that, a mound, but I was beginning to learn it was more than that. There was something under here. The vents led somewhere. I thought about my breath and looked into the kind eyes of my father as he tried to coax from me the truth of what we were doing. I said, "It's hot under here and we let the heat out." I tried to sound smart but couldn't help my eyes travelling from side to side; scared I was getting it wrong.

Dad nodded. He reached down and pulled up a tuft of grass. "You're the first girl ever to do this job and you're smarter than anyone."

I wrinkled my nose. "Apart from you."

Dad shrugged his eyebrows which I took to mean that was already implied. He threw the grass into the air and the cool autumn breeze tugged it off to the side. When he stood, he rested a hand on my shoulder. "Our family has done this job since we arrived here from the north. We'll keep doing it until the giants wake up."

Behind us, far away, another vent choked and tried to close. We made our way across the grass, Dad with his shovel on a shoulder, me dragging mine behind.

Back at the village and Mum had dinner on the boil. I was sure I could smell it the moment we came into the settlement. It was nearly dark, and rain-heavy clouds were fading to black. Mum had stepped outside to look for us.

Mima, my young sister, pushed brown hair from her face as she crouched down in the drain to watch a leaf being carried by the stream. Mum smiled at us as we approached and opened her arms to Dad as he made the last few steps a run. He kissed her before scooping Mima up. She squealed as Dad spun her around. I had a moment of jealousy, remembering him doing that to me. By this point, I was carrying his shovel too.

I squeezed through the narrow door just as a few spots of rain start to spit on me, and by the time we were eating delicious rabbit stew, the rain was hammering on our corrugated iron roof. When it was like this, we just sat quietly and waited for it to pass. Mima placed hands over her ears to block out the sound and pulled a face. We laughed at her antics.

After dinner, we sat round the fire and I told Mum about our day. As I explained about the vents and the heat inside, she nodded in interest and occasionally shared a smile with Dad. I'd begun to recognise this thing she did where she listened like I was telling her something she didn't know but then I would catch her looking at Dad as if to say: *she's so cute when she's learned something.* When she was like this, Dad never tried to bring anything new out in me, or teach me anything. He just smiled at Mum and let her decide how he should think.

"I would have loved the opportunity you have," she then said, as she often did with a regularity I had already resigned myself to. I tuned out though, to the story of fifteen generations since the virus and how our people fled south. They found the giants in their cave and discovered a purpose for themselves supporting the engineers who tended the facility but were too sick to continue. Instead, I looked at Dad as he smiled at Mum as she told us she was brighter than the other girls in her class but she still had to have a family and cook for us while the men did all the interesting work.

I exploded. My anger at that age still surprises me. I'd tuned out that evening but still her incessant going on triggered something in me and I couldn't hold it. "But there are no boys left are there? There's only girls like me and Mima, and one day we'll run this whole place and no-one will ever criticise us for being clever."

Everyone looked at me. Mima was holding a spoon to her mouth and round clear eyes stared blankly at me. Mum just shook her head and sighed, like she was trying to put up with something day in day out. Only Dad seemed interested. His head was slightly bent forward. Light from the fire we sat around flickered across his face. I couldn't understand his expression but in his silence my outburst seemed suddenly pointless; noisy for its own sake. Yet, something stopped me apologising. Mima started chewing again, ignoring the drama. We finished our meal in mostly a quiet and strained atmosphere, until some small talk between Mum and Dad resumed. Mum insisted I didn't need to help tidy up, so I sloped off, upset at this final snub. Wasn't I good enough to do the dishes?

Strolling through the village I heard laughter and chatter, even through the concrete blocks of each building. Cold and dark kept people indoors even though the rain was off. I wandered over to the facility. I could hear something scraping on the pavement before I could see it was Lewis, a boy whose family tended this area. He was sweeping up some leaves from around the wide road leading to the doors. Dad said these were the main doors into the facility, closed for over fifteen generations. Lewis and his family tended to the doors. Even in the darkness I could see Lewis lift his head to see me but he continued his task. Another person ignoring me, I thought, but I continued to approach him anyway.

"Hey," I called out, "You still got some chores to do?"

"Nah, just doing it." He continued sweeping. I stood

watching him. His movements were slightly lit by a glow from the far off boundary lanterns which the picket guards leaned over instead of watching out for bandits. I could see he had that usual scowl on his face he had when teachers, or girls, or boys, or anyone for that matter, spoke to him. Still sweeping, he moved off, so I followed him. The grassy dome above the doors was a black silhouette against the sky. He kept quiet and I never said anything but he kept looking at me like I was annoying him. I was only standing there. What was his problem?

In front of the doors, he swept up the final debris of who knows what in the dark. He blurted out, "Well don't just stand there, give me a hand."

I growled a sigh at him. "Okay. What is it you want me to do?"

"Grab the shovel." He pointed over to a spot beside the door and I stepped over, trusting there was no obstruction to my walking and fumbled about in the dark until I found a shovel. I held it out while he swept the stuff onto it. He showed me a bin where I was to throw it in. He footered about with the bin, his brush, and the shovel until they were all stowed away. Lewis slumped down on the grass next to the massive metal doors. The grass led down from the dome above the facility, the one where I did my work with Dad on the vents.

"Is it not a bit pointless doing that in the dark?" I couldn't believe someone would be out working at night. I looked over to the settlement. My eyes were completely adjusted to the dark, and Lewis had found us a sheltered and quiet spot. It was quite beautiful actually.

Lewis sighed, and I could tell he was aggrieved at my barging in on him. "Nothing's pointless. When the giants awake, we need to be ready. They'll show us what to do next."

"You don't really believe there are giants in there?" I was making fun of him, but I really wanted to know. I could feel the presence of the massive doors behind me, intertwined steel and locked, it was said, with the strength of a hundred men.

"I believe what my old man tells me." He sounded so sure, like his faith in the legend of the giants was pure; untainted by doubt or questions. He spat something from between his lips and looked out across the buildings of our village. Our voices were quiet but they filled this large area.

Without being able to help myself, I found I was pressing him. "But it was his Dad that told him that, all the way back to the engineers we found here, tending this place."

"So why should we doubt it?" He turned to me, and his scowl was gone. "You know the history. Our people fled the virus and the fighting. When they got here, the engineers were few in number and needed help. Why would they lie?"

"But why would we spend our lives tending to them?"

"Not to them," Lewis said, conviction in his young voice. "To the facility. The engineers were not giants' slaves. And nor shall we be."

I recognised the words. "That's right out the school books."

Lewis leaned over and placed his wrists on his knees. "Grown-ups criticise you for not learning while kids give you stick for paying attention."

My own legs were stretched out and I wiggled my feet in response to his exasperation in me. Realising I had been patronising, I changed the subject. "Me and Dad tend the vents."

"Because of the heat inside?"

"Yes, do you know about it?"

Lewis jumped up and told me to follow him. Scrambling to my feet, I skipped after him as he went up to the door. It was massive and don't think I had been that close before. He stood really close to it, and rested an ear on the metal.

He ran his hands over the surface, like he was smoothing a blanket. "What do you feel?" Lewis asked, quietly.

I stepped up and followed his lead. The door was cold against my head. I found myself giggling with a mixture of excitement and embarrassment. He gently shushed me. "You have to listen," Lewis said. "Try it for once."

I tutted but closed my eyes. Hearing his hand slide along the surface of the door like the rustle of grass in the breeze, I placed my own palms on. Though it looked smooth from a distance, I could feel the indentations of the metal, its imperfections and points where the weather had bitten at it. Little crumbles of rust pattered through my fingers and I thought of Lewis sweeping them up tomorrow.

Lewis was whispering now, his gentle voice repeating a fairy story Mum told me and Mima. "We live in a time of legend. Deep inside, far underground, lie the giants. They wait for the day they will wake up and show us the way. We tend the facility, in the tradition of the engineers. The giants watch over us, keeping us safe, and free of the virus."

His voice made me feel sleepy as I drifted into the door, feeling like it could swallow me and I would fall asleep amongst the giants to awake in a place far away, unrecognisable as home. My mind went deep underground, imagining their slumber. Lewis said, "The giants live in an ice palace, surrounded by treasure, guarded by us. The cooling system needs to let out steam, so you open the vents, and close them again to prevent contamination getting in. And far beneath us, you can hear a clock ticking down the time until they awake."

I listened. My head seemed no longer on the door, but beyond it, exploring the passages and I could see a machine, like the clock in the engineers' lab with its swinging pendulum. Yet the one I pictured was massive and filled with wheels of varying sizes. When the hours struck, clockwork people moved inside its mechanism striking bells with tiny spades. And then I could hear it, really hear it, not some imagined sound from my dream timepiece. It was ticking. I opened my eyes and I could see Lewis looking right at me. He knew I could hear it. "It's the giants," he said. "Their breath powers it. No springs, no pulleys, just their breath. You can only hear it from the door."

"I hear things at the vents, but I thought it was just the steam."

I smiled and he grinned back at me. I was thrilled to be sharing this moment with him. Then there was a low thud which seemed to startle him. Lewis jumped back. My shoulder shuddered in fright like someone gripped them as I too hopped away from the door. Clanks and thumps from beyond the door picked out a rhythm in time to the sounds we heard inside. I was terrified. Then we were lit up. Framing the door were a series of rectangular holes I had seen many times, but it was like someone had lit a fire inside each one. They began to glow. A purple bruise at first, the light soon changed to a sort of orange.

I felt Lewis' hand on my arm as he pulled me back but we did not run. The thumps got louder and suddenly steam blew out from the bottom left and right of the doors. The smell was familiar from my time on the vents, a sort of warm water smell, tinged with something tangy and stale. The steam subsided and everything went quiet. I caught sight of Lewis. He looked at me, the scowl back on his face. I suddenly wondered if he remembered the last words of the fairy tale: The time of legend will be over when the giants awake and the doors begin to open.

"What's happening?" I whispered in the darkness.

"I have no idea."

A massive bang, from beyond the door, and a hideous scraping sound screeched out as the doors began to open.

eSOUL

HER SOUL IS in my ebook. When she died, I felt her presence leave the room and the book felt heavier in my hand. Having been reading to her, at her request for her last hours, it leaned into my hands as the weight increased. The room, though, was emptier. It was quieter too, her shallow breathing at an end. Her eyes once looked at me with love and joy. Afterwards, the focus left them, but not before her eyes searched the ceiling like she was thinking of something. She took one last breath and her brow furrowed momentarily. I'd seen this expression before, when she was making a decision about something. Within her head, a thought would pull at her forehead. Her eyes would scan, the resolution was made, she would relax, and she would nod to herself.

She did this when she died. As her eyelids relaxed and, as she made her final breath, she seemed to nod and her body sunk into our bed. People say the dead are at rest but, of course, they mean the body, because the mind goes on, taken on its journey by the soul. I felt it press onto my fingers as her soul entered my ebook. Not yet ready to face the book, and not yet ready to say goodbye to my wife, I placed the device carefully on her bedside cabinet. I let my fingers run across its leather case as I lifted my other hand to her head.

I smoothed out her hair. Already, the heat was beginning to leave her head. We had been prepared for this. My wife encouraged me to listen to the doctor explain how it would happen, so that I would be ready. She sat quietly in the room while the doctor whispered to me the process of death. Like Helen thought it would, I was equipped to face it. Everything occurred as I had been told it would. There would be no pain for Helen, that she would not suffer, that she would just disappear. But she did not go. She's in my ebook.

Her hair smoothed, I lifted my head and tried to take a mental step back. She looked comfortable. Had she been alive, she might have found sleep in such a pose. I pushed the duvet up to her shoulders to keep the warmth within her for as long as I could. She never did like the cold. I lay down next to her for some time until I felt it inappropriate to wait any longer to call the hospital. When the ambulance finally came to take her away, I was left alone with the book. I took it with me when I went to find our daughter.

Sally lives with her husband, and his son, across town and it took me almost thirty minutes to drive there. As I pulled the handbrake, I could see a head bob up at the window. Perhaps it was Sally herself, I cannot be sure, but whoever it was must have known it was me, for our daughter appeared quietly at the door. Her face crumpled as I walked up the path, the book in my coat pocket, and she lifted her arms as I approached. I held Sally as she sobbed. I saw Kevin take young Jason through to the back room. He gave a sad smile and nodded understanding at me. The boy kept quiet, his manners impeccable, as he padded silently away.

Somehow, I moved Sally inside and we sat in her front

room while Kevin brought us tea. Sally must have thought I was being brave for her, because she kept stroking my arm and telling me how sorry she was. I held her hand and told her I was sorry for her loss and the two of us cried sad tears. I would miss the physical presence of my wife, of course, but I would have her with me. I felt the book pull at my coat pocket. Kevin took the garment from me to hang up and I felt a pang of loss as the book went with it, but how could I tell him? I did not then tell Sally that her mother's soul had left her body and was now in my ebook.

Wiping away the last of her tears, Sally found some resolve and told us both that her mother had told her to be ready for that this, that somehow I would not be able to cope, and that she was to help me with the arrangements. I did not argue, not being a very practical man. Sally said she would take care of the funeral. I argued that I would take care of the cost. Despite arguing and saying we would discuss it later; I know Sally will not argue with me over the money. How can a young woman with a young family be expected to pay for a funeral? Besides, Helen had left strict instructions about what she wanted.

Eventually, I was allowed to leave and I went home to my own house. Accompanied by Sally, who slept in the spare room for the first few nights, she insisted on changing the bedclothes as apparently it would be odd not to. I would rather have slipped between the sheets one last time with Helen's scent, not the perfume which Sally thought I meant, by spraying a few drops on the second pillow, but her actual smell. Familiar with it my whole adult life, I would have enjoyed breathing her in one last time.

After bidding my daughter good night, I lay in the bed with the lamp on. I opened the cover of my ebook and flipped the switch. I plugged my headphones in and tapped the commands on the screen to enable speech to text. Helen's voice filled my head as she spoke the words. If you were listening, and had I allowed Sally by my not using the headphones, you would hear only the metallic robot sounds of these devices. But below the surface I could hear Helen. Her soul sang out the words on the page.

At the funeral, we stood round the grave side. It was a beautiful day, with the sun shining warmly upon us. There was a curious tension in the air as the coffin was lowered into the ground. We're not used to this type of funeral anymore, and you could feel people position themselves to see better. No longer able to pull off such physical feats, Kevin, our daughter's husband, kindly took my place. Finally, Helen was at rest as the vicar concluded his part. I threw the first pieces of earth onto the coffin and at that, I broke down. Sally helped me away. My ebook flapped in my jacket pocket.

At the hotel, where we held the wake, I took a chair by the window to receive visitors like an ancient king. I loosened my tie as Helen's sister sat next to me. Mary leaned on me slightly, as is her routine, to indicate her physical presence. It was reassuring and I patted her on the arm. She has perhaps taken it harder than anyone now that her beloved sister is gone. At that point, she was trying to be strong for me, or so she said. Leaning on me was to let me know she was there. Further, as our relatives came up to pay their respects, she fielded some of their thoughts while I stayed quiet. Every now and then I would reach inside my coat pocket and touch the ebook. Sally watched me carefully.

Back home, I settled myself in front of the fire. I didn't need it lit, though the warmth of the day had receded. Kevin made tea while Sally and I sat in the front room. Jason kicked a ball in the garden. Before Sally had entered the room, I had placed the ebook on my side table, ready for a listen later when I was alone. Sally's eyes had fallen on it the moment she came in. She looked like she wanted to say something but thought better of it.

Over tea, we discussed the service and how Helen would have approved. My daughter was exhausted and when Jason came in, he flopped down on the sofa next to his father, he too being tired after a long day for a small boy. I told them they should go home and rest. Kevin agreed, ruffling his son's hair. Jason complained in the way that tired boys do by moaning at his father, who tried to shush him. I found it rather amusing to have a small domestic incident in my lounge. Eventually, Kevin was allowed to take Jason home, and Sally insisted on staying another night despite my protestations.

As the evening progressed, Sally and I shared reminisces about her mother. We spoke of long ago holidays by the sea, Helen's bridge club, and the time my wife decorated a cake for one of Sally's birthdays. My daughter told me she had had a happy childhood and thanked me for it. I was stunned. One doesn't think of childhood as being one thing or another. Isn't it all just jam and long summer holidays? But to hear my daughter's gratitude for something she ought to have taken for granted, though Helen and I did try to make a happy home, to feel the way she did was a marvellous gift to give me that night.

I became rather overcome as did Sally. We sat for a while, listening to the clock on the mantle tick away. Finally, Sally asked me what her mother would say about us crying like old fools. She blew her nose and managed to calm herself. I managed to compose myself and I reached for my book. I leaned over to Sally and asked her if she would like to hear what her mother would say about us. Sally was taken aback and asked me what I meant. I told her about the ebook, a present from Helen, and how at the moment of her death, her spirit had entered the device. Sally went very still. She asked me if I was sure about this. I told her I was.

I opened the cover and flicked on the device. It came to life and I chose the text to speech option. Out came

Helen's voice. Oh, you could hear the metallic, some say robotic, voice that the device uses but beneath it, above, through it and around it you could hear Helen's voice. The sounds rang out around the room. Words and words and words buzzed around me, spoken by Helen, my beloved wife. I would never be alone with Helen here to speak to me. Her voice soothed me the way it did all these years. There was comedy too, a small joke here, and a pun there. And tragedy. All of life is contained in a book and all of Helen was contained in this book. It brought me joy. I looked over to Sally to see her reaction. Her eyes were filled with tears.

CAVALRYMAN

"YOU'RE NOT THE first person to admire it, you know."

Miss Holland smiled at me each morning while I dusted the mirror she kept at head height in her lounge. I always smiled back and said, "It's a very lovely item. What's the story behind it?" She always crinkled her nose up and pointed at the air as if to say I would never catch her out. With this mirror, Miss Holland liked to hint at its secret and tantalise with hints. As her home help, I was the only one she saw with any regularity and I was happy to play along. In truth, I wasn't all that interested. It was just a mirror, shoulder width across, some black spots at the edges and framed in paint flaked metal spirals, the sort of things you can see in houses all the time.

I arrived at her house one morning to find Miss Holland in such a state. She was waiting for me at the door and waved at me as I parked the car. It took me a while to find a spot because there was a blue car in the space in front of her house. By the time I opened the gate and was walking up the path, she was quite panicked. When particularly stressed, her Scottish accent came through quite thickly. "Come in, dear. Quickly. Hurry and find out what he's doing."

Trying to take my coat off, I said, "What on earth has happened?"

Miss Holland tugged at my coat, as if to help me, but I just got tangled. She kept telling me that I needed to find out what he's doing, whoever he was. Her hands touched my arm and they were very cold. I said, "You're freezing. How long have you been at the door?"

"Since he got here, dear," she said. I had to take my coat back off her as she was getting all bundled up inside it. She was not at all steady on her slippers and her head sat an awkward angle because of spine problems. The last thing she needed was a winter coat dragging her to the floor.

We were standing in the hall, with weak morning light at my back. As I closed the front door to preserve what was left of the heat, I stopped. Floorboards creaked from up the stairs. A shadow moved across the top landing. A man's voice called out, "Good morning. I'm Simon. From Walker Antiques."

"He's here for my furniture, dear. Don't let him take my mirror."

Heavy footsteps on the stairs thudded to meet us as is this Simon came down. He was quite young but had that fuddy duddy thing some young people have. He wore an old suit and nervous smile. I was hesitant about what to do. When I had heard his footsteps I had been nervous but he was just some guy. I said, "What are you doing here?"

Simon looked from Miss Holland to me. "I was asked by Mr Holland to appraise some of Miss Holland's things."

"Mr Holland?" I asked him. "You mean Jack?"

He nodded quickly. "Miss Holland let me in. I don't mean to cause distress."

It took me some time but I was able to piece together

the story. Jack Holland was Miss Holland's nephew. I had met him a few times. He seemed nice enough but he always sort of looked around the house like he was sizing it up. This Simon, from Walker's Antiques on the High Street, had been contacted by Jack and arranged the appointment through him. Anticipating his client would have spoken to the aunt, Simon had parked out front and been let in by Miss Holland. This is something I hear about all the time in my job, old people letting strangers into their homes. I was a bit cross with this Simon. He hadn't bothered with Miss Holland's distress until her home help had arrived. So, when he apologised and said he had all he needed anyway, I let him make his excuses and leave.

When I finally got Miss Holland into her chair in the living room, I made us both a cup of tea. She liked me to sit with her after some moments of drama. I didn't have the time really. I'm supposed to be doing some domestic work, not socialising with the customers. She sat back in her chair next to the gas fire and breathed like she'd run a marathon. Sunshine filtered through net curtains and I could feel its warmth but I put the fire on anyway.

"Not too fierce, dear," Miss Holland said, meaning not to put the fire on too high. Her accent was sliding as she calmed down and caught her breath. She was funny sometimes. In normal conversation, her Scots accent faded. And she always called me 'dear'.

"So how do you feel now?" I asked her as she took a sip from a china cup.

"Better thank you," she said. "I'm really cross with that nephew of mine. These are my things. He can get them when I'm gone and not before."

I gave a sympathetic nod. Her house was full of old furniture but doubted it would be worth much. I caught sight of the mirror on the wall to her right. It was set low for her head height. You could see where previous nails had been in the faded wallpaper. As Miss Holland travelled through the years, it had been adjusted down for her. She always looked into the mirror before she left the room. I had seen her do it.

"You're not the first person to admire it, you know," she said to me.

I smiled, relieved at her being back to herself. "Really? What's the story behind it?"

Expecting her to give the usual cryptic answer, she surprised me when she said, "I was given it when I was a young woman. By a cavalryman. When I first came to Oldham."

When she said 'cavalryman', Miss Holland's eyes flashed open for a second. I'm no history expert but I was sure there were no cavalrymen when Miss Holland was young. I didn't challenge her on it, though. Why would I? I did ask her to tell me a bit more, but she pointed at the air again which told me she didn't want her secrets prised out.

Eventually, she fell asleep in her chair. The smell of burning gas made the air muggy and soon she was sleeping deeply, by which I mean snoring. I put a blanket over her knees and turned off the fire. There was still time before the next job so I took to straightening her place up. After washing the tea cups and the few dishes, I ran a duster over the surfaces in the living room. While Miss Holland grabbed some sleep, I had a look at the mirror, having to bend down to see. Its spiral frame drew you in. I saw myself looking tired. I pushed my bottom lip and had a look at my chin.

A shadow fluttered over the surface of the glass, startling me. I stood up and looked behind me at what had caused the shadow. Half expecting Miss Holland to be glowering at me, all I saw was her peaceful living room and her still asleep in her chair. Sunshine still made its way onto her worn carpet. Another shadow flickered. Birds, I realised, birds were flapping by the window causing shadows. I breathed again.

Simon from Walker's antiques didn't visit again while I was there and Miss Holland never mentioned him. Her nephew Jack was noticeable by his absence and again he was never mentioned. Each day I was there, I just did my job. But details of this mirror leaked out from Miss Holland over time. She had moved from Oldham, along with her brother, when his firm offered him promotion. Their parents were long gone and she kept house for her brother. I suspected there had been an Edinburgh sweetheart left behind by Miss Holland, because there was a brief mention of a 'Sandy' but I might be wrong. Her brother married and, as was the norm back then, Miss Holland continued to live with them, even when their son Jack came along. This is where her cavalryman came in.

The story came tumbling out of her as I did my job one day. She followed me from room to room and when I went upstairs, she stood in the hall calling up. Sure enough, this boy was a cavalryman. I imagined the red coats and plumed helmets on fancy occasions but she described him as wearing a dark uniform with shiny buttons. Yellow patches on his shoulder and collar showed his regiment, which was some local outfit still using horses. She didn't describe his face, even when I asked if he was handsome. Over a cup of tea, she touched fingers to her chin and trailed off when she tried to speak about his face.

I let her go quiet but then she said, "He went off to Malaya but before he went he gave me the mirror as an engagement present. We stood side by side looking into it and he said that every time I brushed my hair I would see him right next to me."

How sweet, I thought. "And when he came back from Malaya?"

Miss Holland shook her head. "He never came back from Malaya, dear."

She let that just hang in the air. I knew what she meant

though. Miss Holland looked around the room and I imagined her thinking of all the years from then to now. She touched fingers to her chin again and leaned forward. "Mirrors are magical things," she said. "They have a flat surface but you can see into them. Objects which are far behind you can be seen in the distance, beyond the mirror. Same goes for people. Those who are far behind are beyond the mirror too."

Sadly, Miss Holland died not long after that; weeks it was. I got the call from my supervisor telling me to give that address a miss. That's how you find out. There was no will, but Miss Holland left a note saying I should have the mirror. Her nephew Jack was happy for me to have it, but my employer was cagey about accepting such things. You can see their point. It looks dodgy if you're looking after them in their old age and they leave you things. I ended up buying it, though, from Walker's Antiques on the High Street. In the shop, Simon was very pleased with the thirty pounds he prised out of me. It was sad to see a few of her other things amongst other dusty memories of peoples' lives. Ninety pounds he wanted for Miss Holland's chest of drawers.

I took the mirror home and found a spot for it in the hall. Black spots around the edges, and with its spiral metal frame, the mirror actually looked pretty above the phone table. I could check my look before heading out for the night. As I stood back and admired it, and myself, a shadow fluttered across the glass. I looked over to the front door, the top half being frosted glass covered in a net curtain. There were no birds this time.

Thinking perhaps it was me, I turned back to the mirror and leaned forward. I looked tired and pulled at my cheek to expose a bloodshot eye. In the background of the mirror, I could see my upstairs. A shape moved around up there. Blood drained into my legs. I could feel it. A sick churning in my stomach plunged downwards. The shape moved to the top of the stairs and I could make out it was a man. My throat contracted and bobbed once. I could hear myself breathing out. Moving down the stairs, the man was dressed in a military uniform; dusty leather boots, dark trousers with a yellow strip up the seam and a dark coat with tarnished metal buttons.

All this I saw in the mirror, with me still pulling at my cheek. He stepped to the bottom of the stairs and his face was murky, blotted out almost, by a mist. I let go of my cheek and looked to the side, without moving my head, away from the mirror. No-one there. Turning back to the mirror, the man had moved closer to me. He was still there, in the mirror, but not in the room. A shiver ran across my shoulder and I heard myself breathing out again with no memory of breathing in.

He stood closer to me, this man with an obscured face and military uniform. It was like we were standing side by side, lovers blinking a snapshot for our memories. He paused for a moment, as if hesitant, but then he moved closer to the glass, closer to the real me and his face darkened further. A rage seemed to boil up inside him. He raised gloved fists and started hammering them on the inside of the glass. Despite not seeing his face, I had the sensation of tears, not through anger, but from fear. His fists continued to pound on the inside of the mirror yet I could not hear anything. I was sure he was screaming, yelling his pain, but I could not see the expression on his face, or hear the sound. Imagine dying on a foreign battlefield and leaving this storm behind, an echo in a mirror. I reached up to touch the glass.

But then he was gone. He just evaporated like water spots from a bowl. I breathed in again.

Later that afternoon my own daughter came to visit. As she took off her coat, she caught sight of the mirror. She gave it an odd look and smiled at me as if I had said something funny. I said to her, "You're not the first person to admire it, you know."

"Where did you get that, mum?" she asked, following me into the kitchen.

I filled the kettle. "Your Dad gave it to me before he went off."

She pulled in her chin and screwed up her face. "I've never seen it before."

I plugged the kettle in, and we sat down at the kitchen table. She took out her phone and started fiddling with it. "I know you don't remember him, love. But he loved you. And he loved the horses."

My daughter rolled her eyebrows as she scrolled through her phone. "Horses. Right."

"And he gave me that mirror before he went off," I told her. "He was a cavalryman."

JOSEPH

I HATED MY brother for many years. Anger at the manner of his leaving grew into my despising him. It took years before a day could pass and not think of him. Now he is back and I cannot think of anything else.

He sits to the right of me at the dinner table. Food cools in front of me. Cutlery scrapes on plates. Mary sits to the left of me and compliments my wife's cooking. Beside her Katie chats away to my wife about her day at school. Ethel listens to our daughter but her attention is on me. James, so tall now at fourteen, sits between Ethel and his father, my brother. I say nothing to my brother and have said little since he arrived yesterday. He has taken it for granted that he can stay here in our parents' house and I am powerless to prevent it.

"How was your day?" he asks me. "Was the shop busy?"

Father would have fawned over him, had he been alive, and made an elaborate show of engaging with him about the business. I reply, "Just the usual. How was your day?"

He hesitates. "We visited Mum and Dad."

I take a sip of water and think of the churchyard; bare

trees shivering in the wind as the sun disappears early. Katie stops chattering away and everyone becomes quiet. I glance at my brother. I can see the memory of our parents has hurt him though he tries to cover it with a pale smile. I think of him heading north, with our father not long dead, and my heart hardens again.

After our meal, Mary insists "you men go to the pub", seemingly oblivious to the awkward situation. My brother and I exchange hesitant looks but eventually we agree. Even he thinks it will be difficult for us to be alone. He kisses his wife on the forehead as she does the dishes. We leave Ethel fussing over helping Mary while James teaches Katie a card game in the front room.

The pub is a short walk through the village and it faces my shop. Barrett's Grocers was opened by our father in 1918 when he came home from France. He worked there until his death at the end of the war; our mother having passed on a few years before. When I got demobbed, I took over and married Ethel who worked in the shop. The shop is quiet and dark as we pass by.

We enter the warm air of the pub. From behind the bar, Harry sees us and lines up two pints of export without needing to ask. He is not surprised to see my brother and their conversation shows they must have met again earlier, perhaps today. I pay for the drinks, of course, and we sit down at a small table. We are the only drinkers so far. The clock behind the bar ticks and the fire crackles. Steam vents out a large piece of coal. My brother raises a glass to "being back home" and we sip our drinks. Our local Constable steps in rubbing his hands. He nods a greeting to us but is interested only in letting Harry know he is on his rounds. He will be back later to ensure closing time is observed.

My brother tells me how much he has missed the place and how good a pint you get here. I agree about the pint and say, "No decent pubs up north, then?"

He laughs lightly. "None as good as this."

I wonder at that moment why he ever left and why he convinced Dad to give him cash instead of the shop. Inwardly, I shake my head for his taking Eleanor and James with him. I watch him run his hands across the pub table, quietly admiring the wood. Another man might think me jealous of his skill as a joiner but really I seethe at his constant commentary on timber related topics.

The outside door opens, in walks Jack, and I immediately feel better. He is a big man with a ruddy face and an easy grin. He spies us straight away. "I didn't believe it when I heard." He comes quickly over and shakes my brother's hand vigorously. He slaps me on the shoulder and sends me to the bar to get some more pints. I'm happy to do it. Whilst Harry pulls the pints, I hear them catching up on old times. Jack's laugh is infectious.

Sitting back down with them, we each have a fresh pint. Jack leans his chin on his hands which grip the curved handle of his walking stick as he listens to my brother talking about Eleanor. Jack says, "I'm so sorry to hear about that, fella. She was a lovely girl."

We all agree to that and, a little misty eyed, we raise our glasses to Eleanor and think of her laid to rest in her home town in the north. To take our minds off it, I ask Jack if he'd only just finished work, what with it having been dark for a few hours. Jack takes his cap off and rubs his head. "I came off the hill at about three. I've been up at the big house reporting to his lordship about the state of the herd."

My brother makes the sound of a sheep and we burst out laughing. I realise it is good Jack showed up. We should try and get his brother Frank to join us and the Four Musketeers would be back together.

"And you've got a new wife I hear." Jack punches my brother on the shoulder.

My brother blushes and looks away. "Mary."

We kid him around a bit, saying she's not much older than James, and ask him why she couldn't find some other old geezer to marry. I say, "And her father ran you out of town, did he?"

Jack thinks this is hilarious. My brother laughs nervously and for a moment I think this is what happened. My brother says quietly, "He's a kind man. He gave us some money for the journey, and the bus fares of course."

"Right," says Jack. "And how long have you been married?"

My brother sips his beer, and peers up at the ceiling, making a show of working it out. "Ten months, no sorry, eleven." He looks me straight in the eye as he says it. My blood freezes. I suddenly remember him looking Dad straight in the eye and swearing it was he, and not I, who had left the shop unlocked. He took the punishment that night instead of me.

"And a baby on the way?" asks Jack.

"Due in two months," says my brother. He looks Jack in the eye.

To change my own mood, I dig him in the ribs. "She looks ready to drop any day, son." We all have a laugh about it and enjoy the rest of the evening, reminiscing about our old haunts. I watch my brother laugh at Jack as a story unfolds. His eyes crinkle around the edges like our father's did when he listened to the wireless. I am reminded of his warm laugh, tickled at the shows he loved.

Katie's pony is stabled outside the village. Twinkle the pony has warm lodgings next to two other horses and my daughter does well to keep up with the chores, better than expected. We take our visitors out there for some fresh air. Mid-winter skies threaten rain over steep hills which surround the village. Small white dots of sheep sprinkle the dark grass and I can see two tall figures moving between the animals. "Is that Jack and his brother?" I point up at them.

My brother stops and peers up. "I think it is. Are they coming down the hill?"

"I hope so," I say, slapping my brother on the back. "We'll meet them here."

The girls walk ahead; Mary with her hands on her back, almost waddling. James has stopped beside us. His father is very proud of him. "Tell your uncle what you told me."

James lights up. He has no interest in woodwork like his father but he loves fishing. "There's boats at Loch Fyne that are always needing fixed. Dad could do the repairs on them while I sell bait to the fishermen."

I smile at my nephew's enthusiasm. He's got it all worked out. Wondering if my brother is considering this, which of course means him moving away from here, I see that his jaw has fallen. James is still chattering away. His father's face is ashen and he starts to move away from us. I look to where his attention his; the stables. Mary is bent over double and my daughter is clearly panicked. Ethel is looking this way and she screams out my name. My brother is already on the move and I clap James on the shoulder for him to follow as I race after them.

When we reach them, Mary is in obvious distress. She is crying and clutching her stomach. Ethel is grasping her shoulders. "Give me a hand!" Clumsily, my brother helps Ethel move his wife inside and they lay her down on the straw. Without needing to be told, Katie leads Twinkle out the way. I stand around not knowing what to do. Ethel gives me an angry look as if I should already know what's needed.

"I'll get the doctor," I say and run across the yard into the office where I know there is a phone. I get the girl to call a doctor and hurry back. Mary is on her back with her knees up. Her distress is eased and my wife smiles gently at her, stroking hair away from her damp forehead. Ethel glances at me and with her eyes tells me to take James and his dad out the road. I tap them on the shoulder and lead them out.

As we step away, I hear Mary say to Ethel, "He's a good

man. Most others wouldn't-" My wife shushes her gently and we don't hear any more of the conversation.

The yard has a high fence and I place my forearms on the top rung and my foot on the lowest. My brother does the same while James kicks a stone about, bored already. We watch the two figures make their way down the hill. My brother says, "I think it is Jack and his brother."

I nod. "They'll be here soon."

"Do you think they can see it's us from up there?" He is clearly worried. I catch sight of Katie across the yard. She is in her riding clothes and waves at me as she leads Twinkle across the cobbles. I wave back, listening to the familiar sound of horse hooves on cobbles.

"You've always had a good sense of what's right and what's wrong," I say to my brother.

He pushes himself back from the fence and looks at the ground. His hands remain on the spar and he breathes out. "Sometimes you leave things behind for a reason."

"And sometimes you bring them here for a reason." I'm watching closely for his reaction.

He looks away, unable to make eye contact. "It's not that long ago that a girl on her own would be taken up in front of the Kirk Session to explain herself."

I turn my head away from staring at him, to give him the room to talk, though he says nothing more. Our mother told us about these poor girls, abandoned by men, begging for money from the great and the good of our village, their shame for all to see. I say, "What's right and what's wrong."

My brother relaxes on the fence again. He breathes out in agreement. "And some things are right to do, even when you don't need to do them."

We stand silently for a few minutes. The figures on the hill are definitely Jack and his brother. We can make them out now. Each is wearing clothes suitable for the outdoors, flat caps on their heads, balancing their movement downhill with crooks; tall canes with curved handles made from the horn. I scratch my head, "The four musketeers can wet the baby's head tonight."

My brother chuckles. "We're hoping for a boy, you know."

"Another one? Give me daughters any day." I can hear a car approaching, recognising the sound as that of the doctor's.

He laughs again, freely this time, though he steps back from the fence and puts cold hands in his pockets. "We'll call him after dad."

I smile and rub his shoulder. "Joshua. Good choice."

A black car enters the yard and I raise a hand to the driver and point over to the stables. When it comes to a stop, out jumps the doctor and he rushes in through the open door. My brother and I go over to see if there is anything we can do, though I imagine Ethel shooing us away. Up on the hill, our friends come closer and wave at us, completely unaware of what's been happening as they descend. Jack holds out his arms in greeting, his crook pointing to the sky. I can't hear what he's saying but he's trying to tell us about something he and his brother have seen. James has found a stick and is leaning on it as Katie canters her pony out the yard and onto the bridle path. I hear Mary cry out in pain.

DEMOLITION SQUAD

"THEY'RE BRINGING THEIR own squad in for Japan," I explained to them. "Even after all that travel, the tendering process showed it to be the cheapest option."

My phone rang and I excused myself to Gillian standing just off camera. We had to direct all our conversations to her for reasons I didn't fully understand; something about how it would look on TV. I turned away to answer the call but the camera guy shifted his position. This call had to be good news. Placing my free hand into the big yellow hi-viz jacket I'm wearing, I was very aware of the camera crew bundled into the site kabin listening to everything. I spoke quietly but there wasn't too much to say.

I put my phone away and looked at Gillian. The sound guy listened in on headphones to a fluffy microphone he held just under the camera. His eyes were always unfocused, just listening, while he adjusted controls on a box attached to his waist. The camera guy twisted the lens on his shoulder mounted camera. After a pause, Gillian asked, "Did you get it?"

I suddenly felt quite exposed, knowing that moment

would be broadcast into homes around the country. "Nah, he said the interview was good but they decided to go another way."

"Will there be other promotions coming up?" Gillian asked. Her head leaned forward. She knew this was going to be a good moment for them. They followed me through the application process, from applying online to the interview to the disappointment. This was perfect for them, and for her.

At that time, I didn't know if there would be other supervisor jobs coming up. At that point I didn't really care. "Time for me to go to work."

They followed me outside. How the camera guy got down the stairs with his face pressed up against the camera I do not know. The sound guy was just the same, eyes unfocused, listening all the time. They must get taught it in college or something. I took them up to the gate where Harry was directing the traffic. He waved at us but because he hadn't signed the agreement papers to take part in a reality TV show, he never got to speak.

Gillian said to me, "So tell us about what's happening."

"This is the old JEC building, which produced super-conductors up until the end of last year," I said. "They're pulling out of this site and a supermarket is moving their operation from across the motorway. Once demolished, a new distribution centre will be built right here. Our job today is to keep everything moving."

I helped Harry with the trucks until they had all left the site, taking the last of the people and equipment. Once that was done, we close and lock the gate. "It's all part of a day's work," I said to Gillian and we were off again. I led the camera crew back to the kabin, leaving Harry at the gate, and climbed the stairs. There was a small wooden walkway which we would watch the action on. We were outside the so-called 'Hot Zone' and everyone organised themselves to get a good look at the plant.

Gillian said me, "You were telling us about the squad from Japan."

Now prompted, I gathered myself together. "Yes, they're specialists apparently. The factory is to be flattened to allow the new build to go up."

We were on eastern edge of the old factory site. It was breezy outside though not cold. I pointed out some of the features of the site. Almost half a mile long, the factory was three blocks on either side of a taller admin block which still contained the company logo: JEC. Addressing Gillian, as I had been instructed, while the camera found its own view, I said, "Our job today is to facilitate the security. They'll take care of the rest."

I pointed out that all traffic was being redirected and an exclusion zone set up so the camera crew would be the only and best way to see the action. At the far side of the site, two huge boxes, almost as large as the factory blocks, sat at the ready. The camera guy focused in on them and I went quiet. In the distance, men and women moved about purposefully around the giant boxes. They were dressed in white overalls with the hoods up. Their faces were covered with white surgical masks.

"Is that the Japanese team?" Gillian asked me.

"It's the support team," I explained. I flicked a wrist out and squinted at my watch. "And we're nearly about time."

From a box on the walkway, I pulled out safety goggles and passed them around. The crew were already wearing their hard hats and hi-viz vests but they needed the eye protection. Once everyone had the glasses on, we waited. I thought about it being a Thursday and how the Evening News would be out soon with that week's jobs. I needed something which didn't include standing about outdoors. My mind wandered briefly to what Agnes would think of me stuck on these shifts for a while longer.

"There we are," I said, hands still deep in coat pockets. Beside me, the camera guy adjusted his stance again. The sound guy listened more than watched which was difficult to get used to.

At the far end of the site, some of the support team began to open one of the boxes. "Huge clasps are operated remotely," I said and pointed to a small figure with a tablet device in his hands. "Then they just open the doors."

Sure enough, more support workers pulled at the door until it swung open. Gillian melted back a bit. I bounced on my toes to keep the circulation going. Inside the massive box all you could see was a dark shadow. Something stirred. The support workers stood around for a moment, waiting for something. Despite their distance from us, I could make out one of them checking his watch. One of the others peered inside and impatiently beckoned whatever was inside to come out. A few moments later his voice could be heard, a barked command in Japanese. Then it flew out its box.

"Wingju," I said. I couldn't help smile.

Giant wings unfolded and a massive butterfly fluttered out of the enormous box. Waves of thrust rocked a few of the support workers but they didn't fall over. The camera guy shuffled his feet as he changed his position and adjusted his lens to get a better view. With a wing span of around ten metres, and a length of twelve, Wingju rose into the air. I spoke quickly, "Essentially, a tullerva species butterfly, much larger of course due to the radiation, her long body and small head, for her size-"

"How do you know so much?" Gillian shouted, sounding panicked.

I frowned and pulled back my chin. "Every schoolboy knows about this." She looked at me blankly. The camera guy briefly looked away from his lens to frown and shake his head. Even the sound guy focused on me for a moment. I tried again. "Surely? Tokyo 1956?" They shook their heads and I shook mine back.

Overhead, Wingju gently winged over the site. I could see fine detail in the patterns on her wings. She was beautiful, I thought, more so to see her here than on old news footage. Light filtered through her wings. I felt myself in her shadow as she flew overhead, surveying the scene.

"What now?" Gillian was truly panicking. Her voice had lifted in volume. She pointed at the second box. A technician operated the tablet and two massive clasps opened.

I laughed. Had I got that other job, I realised, I would miss days like these. Support workers hauled back the door of the second box, which was much bigger than the last. I tapped the camera guy on the shoulder, pointed to it, and said to Gillian, "Ganjuki."

She stared at the second box. The support workers stood respectfully back. There was no exhortation from any of the crew, no need to coax this next creature from its box. They waited. From inside the box there was movement. Out of the shadows emerged Ganjuki, a twenty metre tall dinosaur. With slow steps, the giant beast of green skin entered the daylight of Central Scotland. His chunky legs sat atop massive clawed feet. He was balanced by a large tail, which slithered behind him. He stood upright with comical short arms. His head seemed small for his enormous frame. Angry eyes flashed above vicious teeth. Steam vented out nostrils as he snorted forward.

"Oh. My. God." Gillian stepped forward to see better. The cameraman adjusted his position to see round her. I knew what was going to happen next.

Ganjuki stopped and looked around. If he saw his support workers, he did not acknowledge them. He seemed to crick his neck, as if the long journey had made him stiff and he pulled in a massive breath. The support workers pulled on ear defenders. Ganjuki paused and then bellowed out an almighty roar. It thundered out across the site, shaking the factory buildings. We felt the shockwave as our wooden walkway rattled. It was a shout of rage, free of being imprisoned in ice for millions of years, dislodged by a nuclear test. Ganjuki, the creature who destroyed Tokyo in 1956 then became a hero when he defended it with Wingju against the Terror from a Thousand Fathoms. They saved the whole of Japan that day and became poster images for every school kid on the planet. Ganjuki roared again, and rolled his head on his shoulders, a sound which echoed across millennia, this lost soul, the last of his kind.

As the roar faded, I admit to punching a fist in the air. "Now you'll see something." I grabbed the camera guy, bundled him around, and shouted directly into the camera. "Kids! You are about to see something awesome. Hit record. NOW!" I felt triumphant, released from the worry of finding another job, the pressure of being on a stupid reality TV show, and the strain of long shifts. I felt the beating of my heart match the beating of wings in the air as Wingju responded to the call.

The butterfly swopped back overhead. Her massive body swelled with an intake of air. There was a pause and then Wingju breathed out. Fire poured out of her, and dropped onto the factory building, immediately setting it alight. This ignited something within Ganjuki, in the same way it did against the Terror from a Thousand Fathoms, and he stomped towards the building. His clawed feet smashed into the bricks, tearing them apart.

It took them almost a day to destroy Tokyo in 1956, so it took Ganjuki and Wingju a much shorter time to level the old JEC plant. When they were finished, the whole site was flattened. Bulldozers and diggers would only need to prepare foundations for the supermarket distribution centre. Nothing to clear up and a fraction of the cost of a traditional demolition operation meant everyone was happy. Spent from pouring fire upon the land, Wingju floated serenely into her box, ready to sleep again. Ganjuki needed more persuading. A small herd of cows was ushered into the box. The old dinosaur, cut off from its own time, and its own kind, reluctantly entered the box to have its dinner.

I breathed out a huge satisfied sigh. "That was awesome," I said to Gillian. As a boy I had always dreamed of seeing these creatures, an event like this. Because of a twist of fate, I was able to stand there and watch. An amazing experience, for sure.

She looked at me with nothing but shock on her face. The camera guy stayed looking into his viewfinder and the sound guy just looked into the air and listened. Gillian said nothing. She was unable. Like those people to first spot Ganjuki emerging from Tokyo Bay, she was shocked, traumatised even. It was her job to keep her TV show going. However, I guessed it was up to me and I had just the sort of thing the TV people could use. It would show some drama on their show. "Right, we need to get the night shift covered. I'll make some calls. Coming?"

A DAY: IN THE GROTTO

IT'S NOT ALL JAM, you know, getting up for your work in the morning. My name is Elrood, and I'm an employee at the North Pole.

Day for me begins when the alarm goes off. It's always set really early, about 09:00/09:30, something like that. By then, Mum has shouted up at me a couple of times but I usually manage to sleep through that. Breakfast could be anything: cereal, a bit of toast, but it always includes a mug of tea. I would be hopeless without it. Tea is the fuel you need to get through until it's time for cocoa and the sweet release of sleep.

It's not a big journey from Mum 'n' Dad's chalet to the facility where we make things. The factory is underground, with the entrance being an igloo on the surface. I'll head to my workstation and fire up the emails. Despite being sent millions of internal emails a day there are only a few types, and I always answer them in the same way: Click Reply; Type standard response; Click Send; Click Delete.

'Hi Elrood, Would you consider...?' No thanks.

'I'm looking for some help.' Sorry, I'm a bit swamped

right now. Try Flemming.

'Please find attached...' I couldn't find the attachment.

This sort of task is best done whilst having a mug of tea, with one afterwards to recover. From there, it's onto whatever project I'm working on. Our Boss, the guy in the big red suit, will squeeze his chimney challenged frame into your home and deliver the parcels, but it's us who do the hard work. My career at the North Pole has been, shall we say, colourful. It was hardly my fault the property board game had the wrong currencies in them. Only 85% of the boxes were proved to have been affected. Remaining sets are valued by collectors apparently. You're welcome.

My latest posting is a secondment to TRED; Testing Research & Engineering Design. My own thoughts when I walk through the door each day is that it should be called The Room of Eternal Despondency. Honestly, it's so dull. We have to sit and listen to bonkers proposals for process redesign. Everything is acronyms now. TRED you've heard of. RS1 is the Reindeer Stables, all one of them. The MO is the Mayor's Office. Whenever anyone wants me to do something ASAP, it gets done ACOT, After a Cup of Tea.

I thought at first that being on this panel would be interesting, but really it's just a lot of work. We listen to the proposals, read any supporting documents, and write up a report of our findings. Approval finally rests with the Boss but he usually rubber stamps what we decide. So, my friend Jemima and I sit on the board with Bernard, the committee chair. Jemima has been a pal since school. She's famous round here for wearing tartan skirts all the time and a leather jacket, where I favour dark green lederhosen. Jemima rarely wears a hat but I couldn't do without the bell on mine. It's reassuring.

Bernard is a different kettle of fish. Older than us two, he wears business lederhosen. He's the sort of guy who writes to the newspapers about stuff he's seen on TV. In a recent edition of the Chalet Advertiser, they published a long rant from him about who came top in a viewers' poll of the greatest ever singers. Apparently, he was none too pleased Tom Jones came 47th. When he's at work, Bernard has two emotional responses to everything: baffled and undecided.

Our morning session today is to be taken up with a dimbleschpoink this committee knows very well; Horace. Sitting behind our row of tables in the lecture theatre, Jemima puffs out her cheeks and rolls her eyes at me when we realise our favourite inventor is visiting. She says, "I can't believe he's had another idea. I wish he would come up with something we could say yes to."

Bernard sits back in his chair so he can look over his glasses at both of us. His eyes run from side to side. "Now, now. I'm sure Horace has come up with something wonderful. Or at least will at some point."

Hopefully, but it seems unlikely based on his track record. I keep quiet for a change until the man himself comes in. The door opens and in blunders Horace. The bell on his hat chimes out of tune with the ones on his shoes. That's a pet hate of mine. He drags in some kind of contraption, along with a football under one arm, and I quickly make over to help him. It's a mass of metal with plastic tubing. Worryingly, he has also brought a huge glass tube. Annoyingly, I'm carrying the heaviest bits.

"Thanks Elrood," says Horace, out of breath. "Will you give me a hand to set up?"

I look over to the table. Bernard leans his elbows on the surface and cups his hands together. His expression is perplexed. It is against the rules for us to give assistance, but what can I do? Certainly Bernard is unsure of what to advise if his silence is anything to go by. Sitting on her pink tartan skirt, Jemima is no help. Besides, she can't stop giggling as I act under instructions from Horace. We get his gadget together which stands about two metres high. It looks like a rocket launcher designed by a disgruntled penguin.

After I scurry back to my seat, Horace pushes specs up his face and addresses the committee. "Thank you so much for seeing me. My name is Horace and I would like to propose a new transport system for the facility."

Bernard is studiously making notes. He looks up and says, "Jolly good, er, Horace is it? Would you like to demonstrate?"

Jemima and I share a look. He doesn't know who Horace is? This committee only sits for thirty days a year and Horace goes to about forty of them. Still, Horace is quite keen to get on. He goes over to his mass of equipment. Underneath the glass tube, which points at the ceiling, the main machinery has been assembled. He hunts around for a small crank. After turning it a few times, the machine catches and bursts into life.

Over the huge noise it makes, Horace shouts, "It's a mass transport system based on pneumatic messaging systems. Compressed air moving through the tube will move anything, or anyone, you put in it."

Jemima curls herself up on the chair and covers her ears. Bernard turns his hearing aid down. I just watch in amazement. Loud machinery is awesome. This is the most amazing thing Horace has ever brought. I've seen things like this before, for sending small messages in tubes. In fact, we've got one on site. I lost two VHS tapes in one the finance department uses. Horace finds the football he brought in earlier from behind his machine. With a big grin, he holds it up and drops it in the glass tube where it falls to the bottom. Horace then stamps on a big red button on the base of the machine. It suddenly gets louder before it makes an almighty boom. The glass tube shakes for ages before the machine builds up enough pressure. Inside, the football rattles about. Horace looks a bit worried. Something catches his attention. He bends over and pushes a small cable plug into the machine. Suddenly, the football is launched out of the tube. It is propelled towards the ceiling and punches a hole clean through it, taking a light fitting along. The machine stops working and goes quiet. We can hear the ball crashing about upstairs. Someone yells in fright up there while someone else begins to cry. A window breaks. Finally, we hear the ball bounce to a rest like it had been kicked by a small child.

Horace is delighted. Grinning open mouthed, and standing next to his smoking invention, he asks, "What do you think?"

We are still in a bit of shock. Bernard speaks for us all when he says, "I'm not sure where to go with this. Jemima?"

Uncurling herself from the chair, Jemima is a bit more sure of what to say, "Yeah, I'm not getting in that."

Bernard hums some sort of response to her. "It does seem rather, er, enthusiastic. What do you think Elrood?"

It's hard to find something nice to say. I think Horace should have demonstrated it outdoors for starters. Perhaps it would be easier if we had three crosses on the front of our desk and we just buzzed Horace out the room. But actually, I can see an application for this device. If only I could get in it and Horace could fire me out of it. I can almost hear the quiet sound my body would make as I popped out the glass tube: *thdoonk*. It would then launch me away from the North Pole to land in a soft swish amongst deep snow where I could slide into the water and float off out to sea.

"Aah, that sounds lovely," someone says along with a big sigh. When Jemima looks at my funny, I realise it was me who said it. I turn my attention to an expectant Horace. "It's a very interesting device. If you give us any written material you have, we'll be in touch."

Horace is delighted with this response, one we have given him many times. His enthusiasm is adorable. Everyone loves someone who tries their best. Of course, I end up helping him dismantle his machine and cart it back to his workshop. But the good news is: it's lunchtime.

Lunch at our canteen is an experience in itself. Being served today are Blumenhest Burgers, Blumenhest being our chef. If you know anything about great cooking, it's unlikely you've heard of this guy. He doesn't even have his own TV show. Who knows what he puts in the burgers but they taste like walrus blubber boiled in vinegar. I like to tuck into lunch though. Working so hard does that to you.

Jemima joins me, along with Frederick. They pop their trays on the table and bundle up against me. Unlike Jemima in her tartan skirts, Frederick dresses the same as me in lederhosen. The two of them are always together and I have no idea if they are brother and sister, best friends, or boyfriend and girlfriend. They come as a pair, always have, and it seems idiotic to ask now. I ask Frederick how his morning has been. He just shrugs and looks at Jemima. "If certain people weren't dodging out of the real work to listen to crazy inventions I would get on fine."

They think this is hilarious. I do not. Jemima says, "It's only for another couple of days. Elrood will help us pick up your lack of progress when we get back."

I roll my eyes, having no intention of getting involved in their workload. If I can dodge that one, then I certainly will. Frederick nudges me in the ribs. "So, when are you going to enter your invention, Elrood?"

My mouth gives a big non-committal shrug. "When it's ready of course."

Jemima is intrigued. "Have you got an invention you're not telling us about?"

I tap the side of my nose. "That's for me to know."

The two of them give me a big fancy "Oooh!" which makes me laugh. I really do have an invention but it's still at the drawing board stage. It's a range of toys called Captain Elrood and the Soldiers of the North. What I need are quality drawings to plan it all out. I make a mental note to contact a friend in Australia who can help me.

After some more joshing around, at my expense as usual, Jemima and I return to the committee. We settle into our chairs. Bernard is all business like so I try and pretend I'm not suffering from Blumenhest Burgeritis. Jemima gives me a quick smile when Bernard says, "How was lunch at the canteen? I went home and my wife had made sandwiches." He always goes home for lunch, always has sandwiches his wife made, and he always seems so pleased about it.

"Did you bring any leftovers back?" I ask him, but really, I said it for Jemima's amusement. She chuckles to herself.

Bernard ignores me. We call in our next presentation and it's Horace again, this time carrying a single small box. Bernard consults his notes. "Good afternoon, er, Horace is it?"

Unflappable, Horace just grins. "Sure is. And I've got a cracker this time." He holds the box up and his delighted shoulders follow.

I say, "Is it a box, Horace?"

Taking the bait, Horace laughs. "Aha, it is! But inside is something which will revolutionise production round here."

I steal a look at Jemima. In truth, we're very entertained by Horace. He's unbeatable and has an idea for everything. If you were both stuck on a desert island with only a broken up airplane and no means of escape, Horace would build you a recording studio and a spice rack. Jemima says, "Ready when you are Horace."

With that cue, Horace reaches into the box and grabs hold of what's inside. As the box drops away, Horace is left holding his invention. He gives us a wink to show us how proud he is. As one, the committee lean forward to have a closer look. We can't believe our eyes. Horace lifts it up and puts it on his head. He flips a switch and it's activated. We lean back in our chairs. The TRED committee can't believe our eyes. On the other side of the table, in the middle of the lecture theatre, and under a freshly holed ceiling, Horace is wearing his invention.

Bernard is the first to speak. "I say, Horace, is it? This is your most recognisable entry yet."

"Thank you, sir." Horace taps the side of his head with two closed fingers by way of a salute.

Jemima has her chin pulled in. "Is it a hard hat?"

"Sure is," says Horace, rapping knuckles on the invention placed on his head. Sure enough, he has brought along a silver hard hat and placed it on his head. It even has a lamp fitted at the front. When he flicked a switch to active the lamp, it came on. This is his latest invention.

I lean forward and place a pencil I was the side. Even though I've got some questions for him, I doubt the committee will need notes of his replies. "Horace, have you invented a miner's helmet? You know, a hard hat with a lamp fitted to it."

Horace shrivels a bit and seems quite hurt. "No, it's a safety helmet with added luminous functionality."

"You mean the lamp," I say.

Even I realise that sounds like I'm on my high horse, but it doesn't faze Horace. He says, "Yes, but look at this feature."

He makes a big show of holding his head still and moving his eyes from side to side. The lamp swivels along. He looks left, the lamp moves left. He looks right, the lamp moves right. He looks up, you get the idea. Jemima says, "This is awesome actually. I quite like that."

"Really?" says Bernard. "I'm not sure what we would do with such a thing."

Realising Horace is still demonstrating his invention, I say, "Thanks Horace. You can take a rest now."

He stops and staggers a little from being dizzy. None of us help him. One final thing Horace shows us is a magnetic panel on the side of the hard hat. He balances a small spanner above his ear. We make the usual noises about being in touch and let him go. He is grateful for our time and leaves with a smile. I'm just glad there's nothing for me to carry. Horace was able to leave with his invention safely back in its box. And that's the end of the working day. The committee says its goodnights. We meet tomorrow to go over the applications so far, but for today that's it.

After a quick stop to delete the emails I've received today, I head off home. Up on the surface, I leave the igloo with the other workers and make my way back to Mum 'n' Dad's. Passing a tall tree reminds me of something that happened a few years ago. The Boss was doing his usual run to deliver the parcels but he had forgotten one for Daniel, who is one of our customers. He flew the sleigh back to fetch it but, to save him landing, I climbed that tree and held it out for the Boss to catch. It was some climb up that tree and it was terrifying watching the reindeer fly at you with the Boss laughing his head off. But he caught it and Daniel found his parcel under the tree the next morning. What got me thinking though, was I could have done with Horace's cannon. Instead of my climbing that tree, we could have used his transport system to bounce up the parcel. I'll remember that for tomorrow.

When I get home, I go round the back of the chalet. Dad is inside the shed in our yard. He likes pottering about and we often work on stuff together after work. It's my turn to make the dinner so I'll only help out for a short time. I find him fixing mum's bike. He's got it stripped down and the frame sits on the workbench under the shed's window.

He puts a pencil behind his ear and smiles when he sees me. "Hiya son. How was life at the TREDmill?"

"Brilliant," I lie, while Dad laughs at his own joke. "Amazing stuff being invented, Dad. Amazing."

"Give me a hand with this will you," says Dad and he turns back to the bike. As he does so, he bangs his head on the shed's sloping roof. "Ooyah," he says, rubbing his head. "Do you know what I need? A hard-hat."

Something gets my brain going. I look around the shed. It's all quite well laid out with tools and stuff but it's a bit gloomy. I say to him, "You could do with a lamp in here."

Dad chortles. "I sure could." He pats himself down before finding his pencil, tucked in behind an ear. "Have you seen the bike spanner? I've put it down somewhere and I can't find it."

The penny drops for me. Dad bumps his head, needs a lamp, finds a pencil at his ear useful, and loses the spanner. What he needs is Horace's invention, the hard-hat with the swivelling lamp and magnet above the ear. I say to him, "Dad, there's a guy who always brings us demented inventions and we always say no."

"Is it Horace?" asks Dad, almost laughing.

"I guess Horace is well known," I say. Dad's laugh says it all. "Would you test out one of his inventions? It's not much, but we need to encourage guys like him."

Dad looks at me. He picks up a rag and cleans his oily hands on it. He makes a decision. "Sure. I'll test his invention. You fix this bike before you make the dinner."

We shake on it. "I'll give Horace a call tonight and get him to bring it over."

Dad turns his head to the side. "Or take your mum's bike and fetch it yourself."

I agree, reluctantly. When I'm done, it'll be time for cocoa and I'll need a sleep.

FIRST PERSON

"YOU'RE THE LAST to arrive."

It sounds to me more like Jane is giving me a rebuke rather than information. I said to her, "The other six are already here?"

Walking quickly, Jane said, "They got here yesterday, as per the schedule." She was cross with me, but what could I do? The roads were choked as everyone fled north on both sides of the motorway. In contrast, this dry little part of Kent was quite deserted. I tried to keep up.

"We had to find an alternative route," I tried to explain. "And we had to hide overnight-."

She stopped, and I just about walked into her. She held up a hand. "I'm just stressed," Jane said, after trying to find the words. She looked it. Her glasses were a bit grubby and her hair was in an unconvincing pony tail. The overall she was wearing needed changing.

I placed a hand on Jane's arm. "We're all together now. You can rest soon."

She softened, and I saw a glimpse of the old Jane from our undergraduate days. "For a hundred years?"

"Hundred and ten," I said. "If you fancy a lie in."

"Come on." Jane made a fist and bumped the side on my chest.

We were off again, and I followed her through the facility. We were far underground now, having left the British Army's Royal Engineers on the surface to guard us and tend to us while we slept. Technically, we were part of that regiment now, though out of uniform. Arriving at the conference room, I saw that five chairs were already filled by my companions on this journey. No-one smiled. Jane and I took our places in the two empty chairs.

Two days later, we were ready. Feeling exposed in my skinsuit, I lay back in the tube. Jane, equally attired underneath her overall, helped me get ready. I attached the electrodes myself, for the systems to monitor me during hibernation. We were in the hab module. Five identical tubes, filled with our colleagues, fanned out from the central hub. We had monitored them for the initial twenty-four hours of their cycle. No problems meant I was next, with Jane to follow tomorrow.

"You all set?" she asked me.

"Nope." I managed a nervous laugh. "What do you think is happening up there right now?"

Jane sat on the small cushioned edge my tube, fitted there for that purpose. She looked up at the ceiling, as if seeing the surface. "What I don't get, is why the soldiers are doing it."

She meant the Engineers, living out their lives and having families while we slept away the time in deep cold hibernation. Despite their access to a safe place, in a community free from the virus, I too could not imagine doing what they were doing. How would they maintain discipline? Their children would need convincing to keep everything going, and it would be a lot of work over a long period of time. I said, "I mean further out, in the rest of the country. What if they find a cure but forget about us here?"

Jane smiled at that, disappearing in on herself. "That might be quite nice. To sleep until the end of time."

I suddenly wanted to express how I felt about Jane, about our shared career since university, our lives even. For us to find ourselves here, ready to step into the unknown, was quite overwhelming. We told each other we were like time travellers, stepping from now into the future, a hundred years from now. All our families were gone anyway, swallowed in the chaos of the virus. If they weren't gone, they were out of reach. However, in that moment, when I lay back in my cryo-tube and Jane sat on the edge looking inwards, I could not find the words. Instead, I asked her something we and our group of seven already had orders for. "Jane, when we awake, what if the people up there need our help?"

She knew I meant that we would be resurrected from hibernation, perhaps to find the Engineers' numbers depleted through disease or hunger. Morose, she swivelled her eyes towards me. "That's not our mission, Peter. They have their mission and we have ours."

"Of course," I said, not wishing to press her further. I settled back in my tube. "See you in the morning."

The corners of Jane's mouth moved, briefly amused. Her shoulders lifted slightly. Thinking of her next twenty-four hours awake and monitoring the team, she said. "The day after tomorrow for me."

She keyed in the hibernation sequence on a keypad at the top of the tube. Its lid slid over and I felt panicked at being closed in. The temperature dropped.

It's not like floating really. Floating in space while you orbit the earth is actually falling. I'm not falling.

Floating in water feels like sinking and trying not to. And I'm not sinking. I'm free.

Others will surely follow, but not today, and perhaps not soon. It wasn't far, from there to here, but a terrible distance to return, perhaps not possible at all.

I'm not running. Rooted to the spot, I cannot move at all. I have to reach forward and grab the earth to pull myself forward. Before I can progress I must bring the world to me.

* * *

A massive breath in. As if I had been underwater, that breath felt like life itself. The air itself was very cold. I was sitting up. As I tried to steady my breathing, I looked around. Recognising the hab module straight away, it's in darkness. Strip lighting was out. The only light was from a small fluorescent panel in my open tube. I've woken up, I realised. Of course I am, I thought, mentally kicking myself, of course I'm awake. I needed to calm myself and think of my training. Knowing I would be weak, but able to move my arms, I pressed them on the sides of the tube. However, I couldn't get my legs to budge.

I looked around. My tube sat in a fan out of the central hub. Its display told me there was power flowing through. To my left was Alan's tube. It was cracked and in darkness. The glass was blackened and I couldn't see inside, thankfully. I twisted round to my right, in search of Jane's tube.

"Oh my God," I said out loud, as if my voice understood what I was seeing before I saw it. Jane's tube was empty. Its lid was open, unoccupied for a period of time. "Jane?" My voice echoed in the quiet room. "Jane, are you awake?"

I was freezing, beginning to shiver. Shaking my legs to keep warm, I realised some sensation was returning to them. Eventually, I was able to climb out of the tube. Chittering on the cold floor, I found my locker on the wall. My skinsuit was wet and cold but once I'd peeled myself out that and got into my surface gear, I started to feel a bit better. However, tying the laces on my boots was a bit of a trick. I'd forgotten how to do it but I got there in the end.

There was another shock for me. When I checked the tubes, I found that the remaining ones were empty too. Along with Jane, and without poor Alan, the team had awoken and left. I was on my own. This was not the mission orders. We were all set to wake together and head for the surface. Fear pulled at me. I had to gather myself together.

After checking their lockers, which were empty of their surface gear, I left the hab dome. Perhaps they were in the other areas, I thought to myself. Calling out Jane's name, I searched the facility, but there was no-one. Everything was as we left it, though mouldy from time. The elevator was out of power, and access to the stairwell was blocked with some kind of debris, so I had to head for the emergency exit.

Luckily, that was clear, and I climbed the ladder. When I reached the top, I was absolutely knackered. Full of regret for this much exertion so early after waking, by then I needed out. The ladder reached up to a hatch. I was in a narrow tube, so was able to lean back and use both hands. Finally, it gave way and I got it turned. It lifted easily. Light and refreshing air met me as I crawled out.

I was surprised to find neatly tended grass around the hatch. It was smooth on the outside surface, so no-one could access the facility that way, but the area had been well looked after. The hatch sat under a stone pillar, which I remembered from when I arrived. These pillars marked different points on the facility. Placing a palm on the stone, I stood up and looked across the countryside I found myself in. It was England, of course, recognisable in that way. However, I was supposed to be seeing an army base, the one I had left on the surface. What I saw was not that. I was on the grassy mound which covered the underground facility, which I recognised. Beyond that, where the airstrip should be, was nothing but a collection of ramshackle buildings, a shanty town almost.

Unsteady on my feet, I staggered a bit as I tried to move forward. Not wanting to go too far from the safety of my hatch, I got a better view of the buildings. Nothing remained of the army base I could recognise. Some people moved around the shanty town and I ducked down so as not to be seen. I was afraid of them.

Behind, from the direction of the mound, I could hear a sudden hammering. It sounded like metal on metal. I ducked down even further and started to hear a voice, a woman, and then a child's laugh. Creeping towards the hatch, I was moving in the direction of the voices and that metallic smacking noise. I managed to get a boot onto the ladder when a woman's head popped above the grass. She was older than me, with long grey hair which had the odd dark streak through it. Slim and beautiful, her face was weathered. As she neared, chattering away, I could see she was smiling. And she had two children with her, a boy and girl. All three wore practical but worn clothing. In contrast to me in my new army uniform, they were people of the land.

I held my position, hoping not moving would conceal me. The three of them stopped. The older woman held the children back a little. A small puff of steam rose up in front of them and the woman directed the girl towards it. She stepped forward and raised a small shovel in the air before smacking it down on the steam's source. Metal from the shovel connected with metal on the ground. The boy laughed. Steam trickled away. Oddly, it was like they were tending to the facility's vents.

Holding my breath, I waited for them to move off. Just as the woman began to herd the children away, something caught her attention, me, and she froze. Not for long. Lifting her own shovel, she came running towards me with a murderous look on her face. Time for me to go back inside. I shuffled forward to get myself down that shaft to the safety of the underground facility. When I did this, she suddenly stopped. With her shovel full in the air, she halted. Looking from the hatch to me, her expression went from rage to confusion to understanding.

She let the shovel fall behind her and the children jumped out the way. The woman's eyes filled with water. "Peter," she said. The woman said my name. I stopped moving, wondering who this woman was. "Peter," she said again, and passed out, falling straight to the grass.

"My name is Dana," she told me. Her accent made it difficult to tune in to what she said. South-east England, for sure, but the vowels were stretched out further, and there were other flavours in there too that I couldn't place. "Me and another boy were there when the door opened. We were just children."

We sat in her home, one of the brick shanty houses which sat on the old airstrip. After she fainted, the children had become so distressed I felt unable to just leave her there. I needn't have worried. When Dana came to, I helped her back to the shanty town, the village she called it; *viwadj* is how she pronounced it. There were few people there, scared and awestruck by a stranger in their midst.

Dana's home was comfortable and tidy. Her bed was some sort of mat in the corner furthest from the door. In the middle was a lit fireplace and we sat around it on floor cushions, me, Dana, and the little girl. "This is Kari, my lovely grand-daughter who will take over tending to the vents," said Dana, before kissing the child on her head, embarrassing her.

I smiled at this, but I needed more information. "So, when the doors opened. Who came out?"

Dana looked at me, calculating something in her mind. "Three women."

"Only three?" I was shocked. That would be Jane, Terri, and Moira then. With Alan dead in his tube and me still sleeping, there were still two unaccounted for. "Were there no men? Rezwan and Pod?"

She shook her head slowly, a serious look on her face. "Three women only," she said again. "No men."

It was hard for me to concentrate. Thinking of my colleagues waking up without me, the missing two, poor Alan gone, it was difficult to take it all in. Dana watched me carefully through the smoke from the fire. She had been a girl when this had happened and now she was an old woman. Not only that, it never even took into account how long we had been sleeping. Had so much changed in only one hundred years, even with a virus? I had to keep my mind on what Dana might know. "What happened? Where did they go?"

A smile spread across Dana's face. "And you're forgetting why I even know your name."

"Yeah, there's that," I said, throwing a small splinter of wood I had been playing with onto the fire. Seeing me and the hatch, she had put something together in her mind, and called me by my name. I sensed this was the key to my understanding the events that took place in this woman's childhood. Dana whispered something into Kari's ear, and the girl dutifully went off to where the bed was. She dug in behind the head, into the wall. I looked away, imagining this to be some sort of secret hiding place.

When Kari came back, she was carrying a small metal box. Battered and tarnished with age, the box was handed to Dana. The girl was excused by her grandmother and she ran off outside. Dana held the box on her lap, sitting cross-legged on her cushion. She lifted the lid and reached inside. "I have something for you," she said. "From Jane."

It was a letter. Dana handed it over but I couldn't take it. I was excited but to see an aged envelope with my name written on the front was frightening. Dana said gently, "Do you want me to?"

I gulped. "You can read?"

Dana glanced over to the side, momentarily baffled.

"Uh-huh. Don't you? The giants from the past?"

"Giants?" I had no idea what she was talking about.

She brushed me away with the wave of a hand and ripped the side of the envelope. Inside was a single piece of folded paper. Dana opened it, read it, and then held it up to me. "It's only two words," she said, sounding disappointed and annoyed.

I leaned over and looked at the paper. Two words in marker pen said: *First Person.* Dana raised her eyebrows at me and I flopped back on my cushion. "It's our mission," I said, as if that explained anything. "I need to get to Edinburgh, well a place nearby. Do you know of Edinburgh?"

Dana shook her head. From here, our destination by road was over four hundred miles. Who knows what it may be now, what the conditions the roads were in. We were trained to think in miles again, instead of the metric used by the military, so we could rely on road signs if need be. Now that I had seen Jane's message, *First Person*, there was really only one choice. We had spoken about the mission before I was put into hibernation and now she was reminding me of it again. Perhaps there was no way to unravel the mystery of what happened here to my team without going to Edinburgh.

I had made my mind up, and Dana saw it. She said, "Take me with you. I've always wanted to leave here."

"I can't take civilians," I told her.

"What's a civilian?" Dana stumbled over the word. "But I can guess what you mean. It's a term for us folk on the surface that looked after you for seventeen generations."

I stopped her. "Seventeen?"

She glanced at the door. "Kari is among the seventeenth generation, living and dying while you slept."

Stunned, I pulled myself to my feet and fumbled my way out the door. I gulped in air and held the brick door frame. I was standing on the old runway, covered over with this grubby old settlement. Seventeen generations? That could mean anything up to five hundred years, if a 'generation' was between twenty to thirty years. These descendents of the army Engineers, who built this village, had done their jobs for much longer than they ever should. I blundered towards the end of the old runway, to the underground facility. Its massive door was closed securely. I could see it up ahead.

Behind me, Dana called out my name but I ignored her. I had to get back underground, back to the hab module, back to my tube. Wanting only sleep again, I kept going. A few faces looked at me. Dana kept shouting my name. These were not my people. Mine were gone, left behind in the past.

I reached the door and raised a hand to its surface. Little crumbles of rust pattered through my fingers onto the remains of the tarmac at my feet. Slamming my hand on the door, I called out for Jane. Shouting her name out over and over until I was hoarse.

THE LAST OF MEN

The last of men did wait upon the shore,
for their enemy to show his hand,
This final army carried shattered shields,
and tarnished swords of bronze,
after journeys near engulfed by storms,
and fearing Her nine daughters,
would steal their souls and do them harm.

For these are the wars which other men,
would have you fight,
and die and be forgotten,
Or worse, be cursed,
Like that careless King from ancient times,
who let his Queen be smashed upon the rocks,
Her name was damned forever.

Be careful when you stand below those cliffs,
To face that forlorn battle,
and escape this broken land,
you will need the courage of these men,
at this ancient place.

From '*Ragnarok, and other Stories...*' by Wendy Beauly
First published in 1956 by Tea Bay Press & Associates
Reproduced by kind permission

ALSO BY THE AUTHOR

Eizekiel Forth: The Afterlife Detective

The Village King

In the Grotto: Elrood's Story
In the Grotto: Astrid for Mayor

Follow Elrood:
@Elrood_the_Elf
facebook.com/ElroodTheElf

eddiemcgarrity.blogspot.co.uk